DARKE

DARKEST PAST

Haunting Tales

DARKEST PAST

4

In Loving Memory of
Timothy Llewelyn-Hicks

1971 – 2000

The best friend I ever had.

Acknowledgements

Passing Affliction – First published by Written Backwards (Chiral Mad 2) 2013

The Westhoff Version – First published by Villipede Publications (Darkness ad Infinitum: Villipede Horror Anthology 1) 2014

The Other One– First published by Sekhmet Press LLC (Wrapped in White 1)2014

The Setting Sea – First published by Dark Continents Publishing (The Sea) 2014

Alderway – First published by Written Backwards (Chiral Mad) 2012

All of these stories were originally published under the name Patrick O'Neill

I would like to thank the award winning Michael Bailey of Written Backwards for his editing of Alderway and Passing Affliction in their first published forms in Chiral Mad and Chiral Mad 2 respectively.

Special thanks also to the talented team at Villipede Publications (Shawna L. Bernard, Matt Edginton, Alandice A. Anderson and Michael Parker) for their editing of The Westhoff Version in its first published form in Darkness ad Infinitum: Villipede Horror Anthology 1.

Finally, I also thank Nerine Dorman who edited The Setting Sea in the spectacular The Sea Anthology and Jennifer L. Greene who spent so much time proofing and editing The Other One in its first published form in the supremely spooky Wrapped in White Anthology by Sekhmet Press LLC.

Contents

Passing Affliction

Well, here it is: my account as foster carer for the child, Anna Pinter. It won't make for easy reading but then you asked for it, as I knew you would. That's what you social workers do, isn't it? Get it on the record, seal the cracks and make it watertight; a neat little report outlining what occurred, how it all went so wrong and why, but not in your words – mine – so there can be no comeback. You are simply a bystander collating facts, an impartial witness observing events.

I will sign at the bottom of the page and you will file this away amongst the other fragmented chapters – another misfit piece of the unsolvable puzzle, another instalment in another child's disjointed existence in the care system. But this is different and no doubt you will think me insane once you have read it, and with good reason, but it changes nothing. I will recount this chapter exactly as it occurred, regardless of your views.

I wasn't surprised to be selected for Anna's placement. There can't be many foster carers with a track record like mine: 53 placements of varying longevities and complexity, all successfully completed without breakdown, until now. And as for personal experience, having been a wife, mother, widow and childless all before the age of 45 could only have strengthened your case. I'm the one who can cope with problems. I'm the one who can cope with Anna, where everybody else failed.

And how many failed?

I heard that mine was to be her sixth placement with foster carers in as many months; an appalling record for the Borough by any standards. After all, Anna is only 6. But then of course you knew the extent of her difficulties, did you not? Far more than you told. So perhaps your hands are not so clean after all. Your understated summary of her affliction stays with me even now:

"Anna is a quiet child from a difficult background. She simply suffers from an unusual disorder. Shelley, trust me, you are more than capable of caring for her."

The slender file you prepared before her arrival was of equally meagre content, nothing more than a half-filled page.

Name: *Anna Pinter*
Age: *6 years 2 months*
Hair Colour: *Light Brown*
Eye Colour: *Blue/Green*
Background/Circumstance: *Neglect*

Anna is in good physical health although rarely speaks and generally uses nodding and headshaking as a method of communication. Anna was taken into care 6 months ago following removal from the family home under Section 46 of the Children's Act 1989 due to significant concerns around her well-being and of her mother's ability to care for her. Anna's mother is a self-confessed heroin addict and conditions in the family home are of a poor standard. Neglect was clearly apparent. To date Anna has made no mention of her mother, or expressed desire to return home.

And that was it. Not really very helpful. I wonder if you agree now.

It is of no consequence but I remember the morning of Anna's arrival all too well. The house was quiet, unnaturally so, the expectant silence broken only by the monotonous ticking of the grandfather clock in the living room and the distant moaning of autumn wind straining around the brickwork of Bowden Hill.

I have lived in this old house for over two decades now, ever since the car accident that left my life bereft of all meaning, but I have never known a silence like it, as though every brick, wall, ceiling and floor in every room were listening and waiting patiently for her arrival.

I spent the morning making up the long room in the attic. The one that overlooks the lawn to the south. The children always love it here. The walls are yellow and patterned with turquoise and red butterfly print. On the ceiling there are stars that shine and glow through the darkness of night. There are no ominous cupboards or gloomy corners and in the early evenings, red kites glide far above the grass in perfect circles. Sometimes they fly close enough to the leaded windows that you hear their haunted callings. It is a happy room, or at least it was.

Later that morning as I sat waiting, with only the heavy ticking of the clock for company, I gazed out towards the woodland and wondered – as I had wondered so many times before   what it must be like for a child to arrive at this place, so far from anywhere. The potholed driveway, flanked with gnarled almond trees on the approach, must be as daunting as the house itself: red brick against spindly pine trees. Most of the children who have passed through these doors have come from a world where the street is their only knowledge and comfort. They are powerful in their own territory and possess the skills to survive. But here, in the tranquillity of Berkshire's greenbelt countryside, they are suddenly out of their depth, in the beginning at least. It must be hard.

I always try to visualise the children before they arrive and with Anna, it was no different. It is in our nature to second guess outcomes, to speculate, even presume what the future will bring. We simply cannot help ourselves; but how wrong I was with her.

As I opened the front door she peeked up for a fleeting second, just long enough to fix me with her eyes: the right, a luminous turn of pale blue (much like my own), the left, an impossible shade of pea green. Her hair, just as you said, was light brown in colour but so tightly cropped to her pale little head that she appeared bald at first glance.

Her young skin was smooth and without flaw but pallid and translucent; no more than a thin membrane stretched across elf-like features revealing a dark network of tiny veins beneath. I could sense the fear within her as she craned her neck slightly, first to the left, then to the right, to see past me and into the corridor beyond.

"It's alright," I said quietly. "It's nice here. Come in."

I turned my attention to the social worker who had brought Anna; a shabbily dressed effort in his early twenties, perhaps the age Benedict would have been had the car accident never happened.

"You can leave us now," I said. "Thank you for bringing Anna."

I saw his expression change, as I knew it would. He was hoping to have been invited inside to aid Anna's transition to Bowden Hill. Social workers detest relinquishing authority but in my experience their very presence unsettles the children. Through their young eyes, you are the carriers of change, the bearers of uncertainty, and who could blame them? After all, it is you that arrives to 'remove' them from one situation and 'place' them in to another. It is you that threatens their security by forcing decisions that they have had no hand in. They are not stupid. They are children.

I alone decide who steps foot in this place and so, five minutes later, with the wind howling outside and the chiming of the grandfather clock striking the hour, Anna and I were alone.

"It's fine," I beckoned her towards the kitchen. "Follow me."

For the longest time Anna stood motionless on the doormat – eyes downturned, hands dangling limply to her sides – but finally, with nervous breath, she began her careful journey across the hallway, making sure to step only on the smooth grey flagstones and avoid contact with the grout work and cracks in between. Halfway up, she stopped abruptly – perfect black shoes aligned tightly in the centre of a pave – and tapped her palms twice against her hips before continuing.

In the kitchen, she tip-toed cautiously across the tiles and perched herself neatly on a wooden chair, resting her little hands on the table and tucking thumbs out of sight before splaying eight fingers in perfect symmetry across its surface.

Her digits were neatly manicured but the nail on each forefinger had been left to grow and sharpened to a point, like the talon of a small bird. *Why?*

"Are you hungry?"

She shook her head.

"Thirsty?"

Nod.

"Water?"

Nod.

I watched her clasp the glass evenly in both hands and gulp it down. When finished, she returned her hands to the table with spread fingers once again, and smiled a little elfin "thank you."

It almost brought me to tears. She was so utterly trapped. You should have told me. You should have explained and then maybe none of this would have happened.

"Come along. Come and see your new bedroom."

They have a name for it: Obsessive Compulsive Disorder – OCD – an anxiety disorder characterized by repetitive behaviors aimed at reducing fear. But then they have a name for everything, don't they?

The condition is commonplace amongst children who have suffered trauma and neglect, as you well know. And in a way it makes perfect sense. When all else descends into chaos and uncertainty, the establishment of an unwavering routine creates a climate of security; something at least in a world of disorder that is predictable and comforting, an invisible shroud of harmony that, although requiring continual lacing to prevent rips from appearing, fashions a sense of safety.

I could see immediately that Anna's affliction ran far deeper than simple routine though and that her shroud had hardened to an impenetrable barrier between herself and reality, making her captive in a hellish landscape of forced symmetry. Every movement, every action she took was restricted mercilessly by its influence. How I felt for her.

That first night, around midnight, I crept to the attic room to check on her. Moonlight streamed into the darkness and across the butterfly print on the walls. Anna's gentle breaths whispered through the silence at perfectly regular intervals. I had been expecting her to be tucked warmly beneath the covers but instead she lay on the made bed, arms crossed over chest, bare feet in faultless formation, crispy white pyjamas immaculately pressed, as motionless and pale as a corpse.

Later, I took up a tartan blanket and rested it over her delicate form, but when I returned the following morning, Anna was sitting on the bed, arms linked around knees like a little pixie, gazing through the leaded windows and down at the lawn. The tartan blanket was now draped neatly over the mirror on the dressing table, concealing its glass.

"You don't like mirrors?"

Anna shrugged her shoulders and continued eyeing the garden far below.

"Why not?"

She turned then, fixing me with a blank and unreadable mask. October sunlight shone across her pale features, exaggerating further the stark difference in her eye colours. And suddenly I understood: zero symmetry. Why would she possibly want to see that?

"Wait here," I told her. "One minute."

When I returned, I sat gently on the bed and passed her a pair of small mirrored sunglasses. She took them and unfolded the black plastic arms, in and out, in and out, four times, before sliding them on to her face.

"Now come and see."

I stood her before the mirror and rested my hands on her willowy shoulders.

"Trust me."

Her taut little muscles trembled as I reached up and pulled the blanket away.

Silence fell around us like a tangible, vibrant presence and for a moment, as Anna's shoulders tightened to concrete beneath my touch, I thought she would scream but then quite suddenly, she smiled: a bright, wonderful, brilliant smile lined with perfect white teeth.

"You see," I said. "You are beautiful. Anna is beautiful."

I spent the next few days in quiet observation, only sporadically including myself in Anna's games, which usually involved the careful arrangement of toys in neat, military rows to either side of the living room in faultless parallel formation. She sometimes drew butterflies too, but then became anxious if a marking on one wing did not correlate exactly with its counterpart. This always ended with the contaminated picture being folded in half again and again and finally cut in to precise, equally-sided triangles which were then consigned face down to the floor into orderly rows or immaculate patterns.

Having made headway with the mirror incident I was close to winning Anna's trust but knew that it was a fragile, hesitant confidence that could fall away at any time. But I knew that if I could just help Anna find her voice then there would be no turning back. Her speech would be the key. But for now, patience would need to prevail.

I steered clear of bedtime rituals too – even when the distant hum of the electric razor sounded from the attic room.

The head-shaving was an integral part of her routine and, though it went against all my instincts, I knew it would be a mistake to intervene at such an early stage of the placement. I knew how important it was to her. Whilst her eyes were different colours, she could still control the symmetrical appearance of her head. Ironically, I had inadvertently helped her with this particular rite as she was now able sit in front of the mirror, clad in sunglasses, and see exactly what she was doing.

The afternoon that everything changed was much the same as any other that first week. Autumn wind continued to wail around the house like a lost child calling for its mother, spitting rain angrily against the windows. Leaves continued to fall from the beech hedge at the end of the lawn and from the apple tree where the empty wooden swing creaked back and forth. The red kites continued to circle the gun-metal skies far above Bowden Hill and the old grandfather clock continued to tick the seconds away.

At around six o'clock I entered the living room to find Anna sitting at the table by the window, her fingers splayed out evenly across its polished wooden surface. Every so often she would slowly lift her sharpened forefingers in unison, wave them to the left and to the right, and then rest them down again in line with the others.

I took the seat opposite and together we sat for a few moments. Outside, shadows were gathering at the corners of the lawn and a small brown rabbit hopped across the grass and disappeared beneath the darkness of the beech hedge. The grandfather clock chimed the hour.

"Anna, I want you to try something. Something new."

She looked up from her forefingers with interest.

"I want you to turn one hand over, very slowly, and lay it back down on the table. But leave the other one just where it is. Do you think you can do that?"

In a second, Anna's expression changed from interest to fear, her jaw tensing and the glow around her cheeks draining to pallor. Skin tightened across her pointed features and as she shook her head, a small blue vein throbbed at her temple.

"What do you think would happen?" I asked gently. "If you did it?"

Anna swallowed into the quietness and shifted uncomfortably in her seat, first one way and then the other.

I looked at the scene beyond the window. Darkness was forming properly now, gathering in strength in the woodland beyond the lawns. A chill went through me as Anna whispered into the quietness.

"Bad things."

It was the breakthrough though. Finally, she had found the strength to use her voice, the voice that would bring her from captivity to freedom. I could have jumped to my feet in elation. Instead, I kept my nerve.

"Anna, you need to trust me now. You are safe here, in this house. Nothing can hurt you here. I want you to try and turn one hand over. Just try."

Tears brimmed in her eyes. She gulped again, louder this time, her talon-like forefingers tapping nervously in unison on the table. She took a deep breath, crumpled up her delicate features, and turned her right hand on its back.

Silence settled over the room, the same eerie silence that I had felt before Anna's arrival here. But it was more than that, much more, and it took me a moment to understand what had happened, what had changed. Then I saw Anna's eyes turn to the wall behind me, to the grandfather clock. It had stopped ticking.

I will admit, it was odd, as though time itself had suddenly become redundant, meaningless, and that all that was left was Anna and I, struggling to breath in the tense, overbearing atmosphere of the living room.

Then she screamed, a chilling, high pitched shriek that froze every muscle and sinew in my body. I could only watch as Anna clasped her hands over her ears and the sound rose to a terrifying crescendo.

I cried out as something bulky and dark thudded against the window beside us, almost shattering the pane. In the same moment, Anna stopped screaming and ran from the room. The grandfather clock began ticking once again.

Later, I realised it had been a bird. I found its lifeless body, twisted and ruffled, on the grass outside. A red kite.

Throughout that evening I tried repeatedly to convince myself that it had all been coincidence but each time I was left with the same distant sense of unease. What if it hadn't been? What if Anna was right – that '*bad things*' would happen if she did not conform to the symmetry? It was ridiculous, I know, but the feeling would not leave me.

I was slipping on my dressing gown before bed when Anna entered my bedroom with her head held low.

"Sorry," she whispered. "I killed a bird."

"Come here." I put my arms around her. "No you haven't. It was just coincidence. Birds always fly into things. You've done nothing wrong."

I held her for some time. She trembled like a small animal beneath my embrace.

"What happened," she asked quietly into my shoulder, "to you face?"

Caught off guard, I tensed at the memory – bloodied glass and twisted metal, white hot flames and screaming – but then relaxed again, realising that Anna had obviously been wanting to ask me since her arrival. And why wouldn't she? The children that come here always do.

"It was an accident," I said. "In a car. There was a fire."

That night I dreamt of a church, or rather a place beneath a church, far below the surface; a crypt of some kind where an endless corridor of arches stretched out before me and where shadows slid and danced in candlelight. A shape came into view, the pale form of a naked child stepping out from darkness. Anna.

As I approached she raised her face. In the amber glow of the candlelight her eyes were blacker than night. She grinned to expose a perfect set of razor white teeth, glinting with fresh saliva. Pale wings opened in unison around her, their translucent surface mapped with dark veins and ribbed with spiny little bones.

I awoke screaming to the sight of Anna standing over my bed. She was sleepwalking.

She remembered nothing in the morning. Sleepwalkers rarely do. When I went to the attic room she was sitting on her bed staring out of the window at the red kites circling overhead.

"Sometimes in my dreams," she said quietly. "I have wings."

A chill crept down my spine and though it is terrible to admit, in that moment I wished that she had never started to speak again.

It is difficult to explain the atmosphere that dwelled in the house over the next few days. Anna rarely spoke and we fell back into our routines, almost as though nothing had happened. Only now I sensed the presence an invisible void between us, an unspoken

27

barrier that could not be breached. I had attempted to move the situation forwards but that was over now and Anna had retracted into herself once again.

But the retraction was contagious for I too became lost in my thoughts during those long days. Much of the time I found myself staring at the photographs on the mantelpiece in the living room, the ones of Benedict and Charles, mulling over the car accident and everything that I had lost.

Anna continued to play her intricately structured games and to draw butterflies, all predestined for destruction, but I was no more than a spectator on the side lines again. And all the while, with each hour that passed, a quiet but irrefutable tension was steadily building between us.

I was folding clothes in the attic room in early afternoon when I heard the glass smash in the kitchen far below. At first I thought I had imagined it, until I heard Anna scream in pain and begin whimpering into the quiet.

I burst into the kitchen to find her standing on a chair, leaning over the sink with both hands clasped tightly together. She had broken a glass whilst getting a drink, cutting her right forefinger just above the knuckle. Blood dripped through her rigid grasp and onto the clean ceramic surface in large crimson globules.

"It's all right." I peered over the sink. "It's just a scratch. It's not bad."

I should have known not to leave her then – I should have realised – but having seen the cut, which was relatively deep and a borderline case for stitches,

I knew I needed the First Aid Kit from the bathroom, and so I left the kitchen.

When I returned, Anna no longer stood at the sink but was hunched over the now-bloodied kitchen table. The shard of glass in her grasp — poised above the knuckle on her left hand — glinted in the pale sunlight as she went to make the cut.

"Don't you dare!"

But it was too late, of course. She paid me no attention as she sank the splintered glass deep into her left forefinger and dragged its razor edge sideways across the digit to complete the necessary incision in all its bloody glory.

It was not my finest hour as a carer, I will admit, because in that moment I simply exploded — as though all the tension that had built in the past few days had finally burst through the vents and found a way into the open.

I called her 'stupid' and 'bad' and 'ridiculous'. All of the things one should never say to a child. It was a terrible, violent and unforgivable verbal attack of which I am deeply ashamed.

Afterwards, I apologised profusely and washed and bandaged her little fingers with gorse and tape to stop the flow of blood, but I could see that it was no use. Anna had withdrawn into herself further still and I knew that this time it would be virtually impossible to coax her back out again. What little trust I had built, was gone. She could barely meet my eyes.

As I sat in the living room hours later, watching Anna swaying back on forth on the swing beneath the apple tree outside − with perfectly aligned hands on the chains − I cried.

Though she had her back to me as she rocked to and fro and was facing the hedge at the end of the lawn, I felt somehow she knew I was watching. Every now and then she would lift two bandaged fingers in perfect symmetry and then rest them down again as she swung.

I sat there for some minutes, mesmerised by the motion of the swing, by her small silhouette swaying in the shadows of the gnarled branches but then, it began.

Anna lifted her right arm horizontally, using the other to hold the swing steady. As she swung, asymmetrically, the grandfather clock stopped.

Coincidence, surely. But as Anna lifted her leg out straight before her and tucked the other beneath the swing, the living room door slammed into the silence and the photograph of Benedict and Charles fell from the mantelpiece and shattered to the floor.

Outside, the wind picked up as Anna swung higher and higher. She had pulled the chain hard on one side to make the swing twist unevenly as she rode. The pine trees on the edges of the lawn creaked and bowed. Dead leaves blew out from the woodland and danced on the grass before her. Through the gale, and just as the window beside me shattered, I thought I heard the shrill sound of her laughter.

A terrible realisation: it was not the affliction that controlled Anna, or the fear, but rather that Anna was in complete control and always had been. Not the slave, but the master.

But enough was enough.

It took only moments to crunch across the broken glass of the living room and yank open the door to the garden. Head down to the wind, I tore across the grass and wrenched Anna from the swing.

She wriggled and kicked and screamed in my arms as I bundled her roughly back to the house and forced her to sit at the kitchen table.

"This stops here," I yelled, ripping a chair across the floor for myself. "Right now."

Anna fixed me with a fierce stare, laced with malice and, as I sat before her, something in her bizarre and wild eyes sent an icy chill to my soul, not the eyes of a child, but the eyes of something else altogether.

"You can't change me," she whispered loudly. "Just the same as you can't change that you were driving the car that day."

I stopped then because, suddenly, I had nothing more.

The shock of what she had said cut deeper than any knife could have. She was right of course, but to hear it like that. There was no way she could have known.

"But I can change *you*." She grasped my limp hands and grinned at me as the razor nails of her forefingers pierced the skin of my knuckles and drove down into the bone.

It is difficult to recall, but I do remember the coldness rushing up my arms, my neck, through my blood and around my body until paralysis set in. I thought I heard wings flapping about me, and a terrible screeching noise that made me think of the red kites above the house. Was it me screaming or something else?

But it is all finished now. The placement has failed and no doubt you have secured the services of another carer for Anna. I wonder if you provided the same inadequate information to them, or whether you thought it right to explain in detail this time. I'd put money on the former.

As for me, I am becoming used to it now, the rules and boundaries to which I must abide. The importance of symmetry and routine are supreme and overriding. I know exactly what I must do to keep disorder from creeping in. The affliction has been passed in its entirety. Mirrors are becoming difficult. My left eye is changing – an impossible shade of pea green – and when I stare into the glass the lack of equilibrium is creating problems. Sunglasses help but the facial scarring from the accident is not so easily rectified. I have made new incisions and burns but it could be years before the results become acceptable.

I am a mere novice but I will learn as time passes, perhaps even control in the end, the force that waits to be unleashed.

So go on, file this away with the other chapters, as you will. But do not send any more children here. It is not safe.

The Westhoff Version

"Dad, what's foie gras?"

It had been a long night, lost in blurring hours of darkened motorway and streaming white lines. We had driven out of Cherbourg and headed south through the night towards Nantes, then further still past Bordeaux, only stopping to refuel or take toilet breaks. We were destined for Masseube, or rather a remote farmhouse with Masseube as its nearest point of significant civilization. We had planned to share the driving but sometime after midnight Kelly had fallen asleep and not come around again.

Until now, Joseph had slept most of the way too.

Near our destination, the roads narrowed and dipped in and out of valleys. On the edge of the horizon, the snow-capped peaks of the Pyrenees were silhouetted against the first hesitant shades of dawn. But even in the early hours, the air was warm here and, as rolling landscapes carpeted with dying sunflowers steadily emerged from darkness, I began to realize just how secluded our holiday location would be. Every now and then the headlights picked out battered wooden signs with the words *foie gras* scrawled across them in painted letters.

There was no way I would have found this place without satellite navigation.

"Dad?"

I had been hoping Joseph would fall back to sleep, but there was no chance of that now. He was eleven and eager to begin our summer holiday. He had seen the pictures: the swimming pool, the snooker table, the ping pong set. And now, as morning light grew in strength, there was no way he would sleep again.

"You're sure you want to know?" I asked. "It's pretty horrible."

This ignited interest, as I knew it would, and he craned his neck between the seats to hear the explanation.

"Foie gras means, *fat liver* – and you eat it. It's actually made of duck's liver."

"Urgh."

"Disgusting, hey? But it gets worse than that, you know why? Because of how they make it. You want to know how they make it?"

Joseph smiled at me from between the seats and nodded slowly.

"Well, first they get the duck and they put it in a metal cage. But it's not a normal cage. It's a really small cage with a big hole at the top so the duck can stick its head out. But the cage isn't just *small* – it's so small that the duck can't even move. In fact, the only thing it can do is move its head."

"Why do they do that?"

"Well, if the duck can move it means it can exercise, like a duck is supposed to, right? But they don't want that. They want the duck to stay exactly in the same position and get fat. And so they feed it and feed it and feed it every day through a tube down its neck, and in the end that makes its liver all fat and swollen up. And when it's fat and swollen up enough, they kill the duck and make its liver into a nice pâté so they can eat it."

"Who are *they?*"

"Tom, that's enough." Kelly was suddenly awake next to me. "That's a horrible thing to tell a child. Absolutely horrible. What is wrong with you?"

"Look. I'm just telling him how it is. He's old enough to hear these things now."

"Yeah, Mum. I am old enough, you know."

A long silence followed. I had inadvertently managed to do it again: pit the boys against the girls. But therein, as always, lay the problem – there was two of us, and only one of her.

"You're right," I said. "I'm sorry."

"Mum, have you ever eaten foie gras?"

"No, I have not."

"Dad, have –"

"Wait. This is it."

The sunflowers had given way to bare, unfarmed land, and the road narrowed to a small junction where a crumbling memorial rose from the dried earth like a Norse god silently watching over the landscape. Beyond this, the ruined chapel of Le Carde stood derelict amongst crooked headstones and rusting crucifixes. I recognized it all from the photographs. Our destination was less than a hundred meters from this place.

Isolated from the road by a gravel driveway, the farmhouse was exactly as I had imagined. Set on one level, it looked over the chapel of Le Carde and across the hills beyond, its pale structure lined with dark veins of stained oak. I found the keys amongst the bright flowers in the ornamental cartwheel that lay beside the pond, just as we had agreed with the owners. My legs ached from driving and I felt like hell. We had arrived, and I was done.

"I have to sleep."

Hours later, I woke to the comforting sound of Joseph splashing in the pool, warm French sunlight beaming on my face from the skylight above the bed. I knew we had nothing in the house and that I would need to get the local village of Masseube to pick up essentials, so I got up straight away. Joseph got dry and dressed quickly, unable to contain his curiosity to explore the locality. Within minutes we were on the road again, crossing the eight kilometres towards the small settlement and leaving Kelly to sunbathe beside the pool. We were halfway there when I realized the satellite navigation had stopped working.

Nevertheless, we had no trouble in finding the supermarket outside Masseube, which was well marked and larger than I had expected. Simply stepping out of the sunshine and into its air-conditioned coolness made me feel exhilarated for the first time since arriving. Alongside the wine, cheeses, and fresh bread, we crammed the trolley with unnecessary treats and I made the mistake of telling Joseph that he could have whatever he wanted.

When he returned, he was grinning and holding a jar of foie gras. I made him put it back on the grounds that it was too expensive, but part of me wanted to buy it because I knew exactly what he would have done with it. He would have taken it back to England, carefully wrapped in clothes, where it would have taken pride-of-place on the *special shelf*; that most hallowed of all sanctuaries, reserved only for the most bizarre and exotic trophies from across Europe and beyond: the clear vodka lollipop, complete with scorpion inside; the shiny remains of a long-dead stag beetle; a dried, baby crocodile, and finally, the foie gras – in all its glory – potted in glass with roughly-woven sacking fastened about its neck by a ribbon. But it was not to be.

While checking out, I asked in staggered French for directions to Le Carde because I knew I would struggle to find the farmhouse again without satellite navigation. The girl behind the register drew a map and gave it to Joseph with a kind smile.

When we got back in the car, I noticed a little old French woman who I immediately recognized from the supermarket queue hobbling towards us, carrying shopping in one hand and waving frantically with the other.

"What does she want, Dad?"

I opened the window as she approached. Her hands were gnarled with arthritis but her dark eyes caught me with an unnerving intensity. When she spoke, she did not blink.

"Monsieur, faire attention. Il ya des serpents sur les collines dans Le Carde. Il n'est pas sur. Il est très dangereux," she pointed to Joseph in the backseat with a twisted finger, " . . . pour l'enfant."

I thanked her hastily and drove away in the direction of Le Carde. In the rear view mirror I could see the old woman standing alone in the supermarket car park, pale faced and hunched, staring on at us intently.

"Dad, she was creepy. What did she say?"

"She said there are snakes on the hills in Le Carde. And that we need to be careful, because it's dangerous."

We drove in silence for a time. In the back seat, Joseph had rolled down the window and was staring at the dried foliage on the verge as we passed the sunflower fields. He was looking for snakes. Less than a kilometre from the farmhouse, he called out.

"Dad, behind us!"

I barely had time to check the mirror before the Daimler was right up against us.

Up ahead, the road meandered to a blind corner, but I instinctively knew what was about to happen. The Daimler silently accelerated and came alongside us, passing in a blur of tinted glass and black metallic paint. I caught a fleeting glimpse of the driver: a silver-haired man with sharp nose and high cheekbones. But almost in the same instant, the car was gone, into the blind corner and out of sight.

Later that evening, after we had eaten and Joseph was taking a final swim with Kelly, I wandered to the end of the driveway and leaned against the wall to light a cigarette. From here, and at this time in the evening before sunset, the countryside was absolutely still. At the very edge of a wooded area across the dry landscape, a motionless deer stood in a parched field. Far above it, a solitary bird of prey circled the area. A warm breeze stole across the fields for a moment, carrying the scent of dry earth and sweet wild flowers.

And then I saw it for the first time: the other farmhouse, across the fields, half-hidden by tall fir trees. I could see that it was accessible from a track that snaked past the chapel ruins and down into the valley to the other side. The black nose of the Daimler poked out from the side of the house and, though the fir trees offered only a limited view, I could see the thin silhouette of a man standing on the main lawn, staring back at me. In the stillness, he raised a hand and waved once.

I did the same, and we stood motionless for some seconds before I turned and walked back to the house. It was a strange moment. It stays with me, even now.

Later, when Kelly and Joseph were sleeping, I strolled down to the wall again, where a faux Victorian lamp post cast a pool of amber light over the entrance to the driveway. Bats flickered in and out of its humming brightness, undisturbed by my presence. Across the fields, the lights from the other farmhouse shone out like a skeletal face leering across the blackness of the valley.

I began to relax properly over the next few days. In the period leading up to the holiday, I'd barely had a moment for Joseph. A sudden dip in the markets had caused a flood of investors to buy at what they considered to be a "low point", and we had struggled to make all the trades before the inevitable upturn began. But now, far away from anywhere, in the warm sunlight, I could forget all about the mundane and repetitive world of finances and concentrate instead on the important things: ping pong, swimming, and snake-hunting with Joseph.

Kelly and I hadn't taken a week's holiday in over three years and we were loving every second. The accommodations were basic — the furniture a mismatch of different styles and ages, the kitchenware a senseless combination of random sets – but it was all perfect for us. All we needed was the sunshine, and each other. It was bliss.

I always knew that the French were keen on recycling, so it was no surprise to find the collection of communal wheelie-bins parked behind the ruined chapel: green for bottles, red for cans and plastic, black for household waste.

The clouds had thickened that morning and hung like the belly of a huge grey beast over the fields. The humidity was high and had brought with it an unpleasant stillness that seemed to make the flies more active, especially in the dusty clearing around the bins. I brushed them from my face as I clanked empty wine bottles into the quietness. From where I stood I could see the crumbling headstones and jagged iron crosses in the shadow of the ruins. There was a terrible smell about the place; not just the smell of rubbish, but something else beneath that – a sweet and nauseating stench – like the smell of rotten meat. I was about to close the bin lid when I heard a voice behind me.

"Good morning."

I turned to see the black Daimler parked in the road. The driver's window was open and inside a dark-haired woman smiled from behind large, bug-like sunglasses. I took her to be around sixty-five, although it was hard to tell given the amount of pale makeup covering her face.

"Judith Westhoff." She reached out her hand. "From the farmhouse across the fields. How are you settling in?"

"Pretty well, thanks. I'm Tom." I shook her hand, which felt oddly wet and boneless beneath my grip and made me want to pull away immediately. She removed her sunglasses and peered with concern across the cemetery.

"The rain's coming. It's always like this before the rain. I *so* hope it does. It's been twenty-three days now."

I could see her more clearly now: grey roots against black hair-dye, eyes a fresh marine colour that belonged to someone far younger.

"Yes, it certainly needs –"

"Morris and I were wondering if the three of you would like to come around to the house tonight," she interrupted suddenly. "For drinks. We could tell you all about the area. We're easy to find – just walk around the track to other side of the valley and we're there on the left." She pointed through the tinted glass of the Daimler to the fields beyond.

"Okay. I mean, yes that would be lovely. Thank you."

"Excellent. Let's say seven, then?"

Soon afterwards the Daimler purred away, leaving me standing in a cloud of swirling dust. I thought for a moment as the sky darkened that rain would come, but it did not.

Back at the poolside, I told Kelly about the invitation.

"I cannot believe you agreed to that without talking to me first. Did it even cross your mind that maybe – just maybe – I would not want to spend the second last evening of our holiday doing *that*?"

"Oh, come one. It's just for an hour. Where's your sense of adventure?"

"Yeah, Mum," Joseph said, pulling himself out of the pool. "It might be fun."

Kelly stood up and wrapped a towel tightly around her waist. It was impossible to ignore the sarcasm in her voice.

"I tell you what then," she said as she walked away from us. "Why don't we just take a vote? That would be the fairest way, wouldn't it?"

By six-thirty, all three of us were dressed and ready. Kelly was wearing a loose white top and jeans. I had forgotten how beautiful she was with a tan; the way it lifted her green eyes. Joseph had copied me to the letter in beige shorts and a navy blue t-shirt. He had even combed his dark hair back and used my gel to realize the most perfect imitation ever.

We locked up the house and walked slowly in the oppressive heat, past the war memorial and towards the ruined chapel of Le Carde. Joseph raced on ahead to get there before us and Kelly stopped and turned to me.

"I'm sorry," she said. "I was wrong to react like that before. It's just that I've loved it so much here, just the three of us. It's been perfect. I couldn't bear to think of anything spoiling what we've had. I am sorry. And I'm sure it will be fun too."

She reached out and touched my face. We kissed tenderly for a long moment, and then continued towards the chapel.

We took a break when we reached the dilapidated wall of the cemetery so that we could take a proper look. The structure of the chapel remained more or less intact, although the roof was collapsed and dried ivy tendrils crept from its shadowy interior and flowed over its thick, flint walls. The cemetery was a mess of brambles and reeds. Fragmented gravestones rose from the foliage and only glimpses of the fractured soil could be seen beneath. The scent of old death hung in the warm air.

"It must have been like this for decades," I said, wiping sweat from my forehead.

"I don't think so," Kelly replied quietly, as though worried she may disturb the quietness around us. "Look."

She was pointing to a clearing in the brambles where, beneath a crumbling headstone, the soil was darker and did not have the same line-cracked quality as the rest. There was no doubt the earth had been disturbed there.

"Dad, check it out."

I turned to see Joseph gazing into the distance where black clouds had gathered over the jagged outlines of the Pyrenees. Tiny veins of lighting flickered intermittently from the darkness and into the mountains. A flock of white geese flew overhead in formation, winging away from the storm. One cried out like a child in terrible pain.

"It's coming our way," I said. "Come on, let's get going."

The Westhoff residence was bigger than I had imagined. As we crunched along the gravel driveway beneath the fir trees, lawns rolled out before us, perfectly trimmed and impossibly green. The swimming pool looked brand new, too. Swallows glided down to skim its surface before rising up again into the heavy skies.

"Dad, what's that?" Joseph had stopped and was looking at a large wicker object at the edge of the lawn.

"It's a lobster cage," I said. "They use it to catch lobsters."

The house itself was constructed in a similar style to the one we had rented − red brick with oak−stained beams lining its breadth − Tudor in style, but on two levels. The windows were leaded in the traditional style but looked new. They had spent money here.

As we approached, Judith Westhoff appeared in the doorway to meet us. I introduced Kelly and Joseph before we were ushered into a wood−panelled hallway adorned with stuffed deer heads and antelope horns. I looked at Joseph, who was smiling in bewilderment at it all.

"This way," said Judith. "Just through here now."

I hadn't realized until now just how tall she was, and how thin. Her black evening dress hung loosely from her shoulders. She wore thin gold jewellery about her wrists and neck. Wafts of floral perfume lingered in the air as we followed her beneath an old stone archway and out onto the patio behind the house. I saw again the grey roots at the base of her hair as we stepped into the dim light, and it struck me that, in spite of the expensive surroundings, she probably didn't entertain very often.

From the patio, the view to the mountains on the horizon was breathtaking. Fields overlapped one another in pale shades of amber and green. Farmhouses and dilapidated outbuildings lay scattered around the valleys like broken bones. The storm was edging closer now. The first fragmented rumbles of thunder sounded across the landscape.

"It's beautiful," Kelly said. "Stunning."

At the far end of the patio, where the view was best, a white table bore wine glasses, canapés and clean plates, all sheltered beneath a pale blue parasol.

A man's voice sounded behind us.

"Yes, we are lucky here. Very fortunate indeed. You missed the sunflowers, though. A month ago the world was yellow."

Morris Westhoff was a small man with thick silver hair and high, feline cheekbones. His linen suit flapped about his thin frame as he approached us. He smiled to expose a perfect set of white teeth that spread impossibly across his tanned features.

Judith poured red wine and gave Joseph lemonade with ice. I left Kelly and wandered to the edge of the patio with Morris.

He explained that they had bought the house just over six years ago, after he had retired from his career as a Research Scientist at a cosmetics laboratory in Berkshire. I asked him if he missed England.

"God forbid! Look around. What could we possibly want for?"

I shared my views on current market trends and the world economy at large. Morris listened intently, taking in every word from behind small grey eyes. I got the feeling he enjoyed significant wealth and investment experience. His questions were detailed and company specific. In truth, I struggled to keep pace with them, as he must have known.

"The wine is fantastic," I said as he refilled my glass.

"It's the local drop. Very good, I agree. Try some cheese."

I thanked him and took a cracker with Roquefort.

"They certainly get it right with the cheeses and wines," he said, "but to my mind they fail abysmally on the cooking side."

Just then, Kelly and Joseph came over to join us. I put an arm around Joseph and smiled as Morris continued.

"For example, have you tasted the local duck foie gras?"

"No," I replied. "I can't say I have."

"Ah, well in that case, you must try some."

"That would be lovely."

I smiled over at Kelly who was staring hard at me with serious green eyes.

"When in France . . ." I said to her quietly.

"Judy, darling," Morris called out. "Bring out the foie gras, please."

I excused myself to find the toilet on the ground floor, which was situated off the main entrance hall.

Inside, the walls were clean and white. A solitary colour photograph hung in a wooden frame above the sink – a portrait of Morris many years earlier – dressed in a clinical white lab coat, smiling his wide smile at the camera, all-white teeth showing. In the background, wire cages were stacked on either side of the corridor behind him. The face of a small monkey peered out from one of them, a forlorn expression stretched across his face. Until that moment, I hadn't really considered what being a Research Scientist for a cosmetics company actually meant.

"Now, here we are," Morris said as I joined the group again.

The table beneath the parasol had been cleared now except for two plates. A pale round slice of foie gras sat on each. Joseph craned his head to take a closer look, then moved away again as the rich scent caught his nostrils.

"Would you like some, dear?" Judith asked. "It's very tasty."

"No, thank you." Joseph recoiled in a clumsy backwards step. "I don't want any at all, thank you."

"Ah, now that is a shame. You look like you could do with some fattening up. How about you, Kelly?"

"I won't. Thank you, Judith, but I disagree with it entirely."

Morris cast a quizzical look in her direction. "What is it exactly that you disagree with, Kelly?"

"The way it's made is cruel and inhumane. I don't know how anyone could eat it."

"And yet we accept the idea of fattening turkeys for Christmas," Morris said, raising a silver eyebrow, "and all of the chickens that line our supermarket shelves."

"It's different," Kelly said evenly. "They're not force fed."

"Oh, is that so?" Morris nodded and smiled to himself. "That, I did not know."

A long silence followed and Kelly gave me her best *Can we leave now please?* look. I was surprised at how quickly Westhoff had rattled her. The thunder made itself known again, louder this time, like a train battering towards us from behind the dark clouds. Lightning blinked on the horizon and Morris clapped his hands together firmly.

"Right then. To prove my point, try this one first. The local foie gras."

I took the plate and carved a small amount of the supple pâté onto my spoon. Joseph's eyes were fixated on me with a mixture of excitement and horror as I raised it to my mouth. The flavour was creamy and rich and smooth, with the faintest under-taste of liver. It dissolved away like butter on the palate, leaving a tingling sensation on edges of my tongue.

"I'm sorry, Morris," I said. "But I think that's actually very good."

He raised a small hand to quiet me before passing me the other plate.

"Now, try this one."

This pâté, a paler shade of pink than the first, was oval in shape, with a small, red trim of fat about its circumference. I knew from the moment my spoon cut effortlessly through its tender consistency that it would be even more delicate and buttery than its predecessor. As I put the spoon into my mouth, I saw that Morris was staring at me intently.

His grey eyes narrowed and a trembling, half-smile played around the edge of his thin lips. A small fly crept across his smooth brown skin before settling on the end of his nose, but he did not notice. Small beads of sweat had formed on his brow; one trickled down and landed in a dark stain on his perfect linen suit.

The taste was extraordinary: smooth and rich once again, but the under-taste of liver was a barely detectable dimension beneath the buttery, exquisite texture which melted away on my tongue in seconds. I had never tasted anything like it.

"That is possibly the most beautiful thing I have ever tasted."

Morris clapped his hands together in delight. The smile was back now, wider than ever, and I realized suddenly that the teeth were simply too white, too wide, and too flawless to be anything other than dentures.

"The first foie gras, as I have already explained, is the local attempt," he said. "The second however, is the Westhoff version, and, dare I say it, the *correct* version - created right here beneath our very feet."

"You made this?"

Morris nodded proudly, resting hands on his hips and pointing his beige brogues east and west.

"Foie gras is simply fat held together and flavoured by what was once the liver.

Essentially, it's all about this semi-solid fat -which, though neutral to the taste, is slightly meaty. If executed correctly, the solidification point of the fat is such that it melts on the tongue, going from solid to liquid with the body's temperature, just as it's eaten – hence the *melt in the mouth* sensation. Now, the French do understand this – I have no doubt – but they have failed in the most fundamental way. Their basic ingredient is wrong."

Just then, Judith appeared on the patio.

"Morris, I'm sorry to interrupt, darling, but have you fed the kids yet this evening?"

Silence was again broken by the distant rumbling of thunder. Judith smiled on at us, and I noticed that her unnaturally blue eyes had changed somehow. Was it possible she was wearing coloured contacts? Yes, I could see it now. The blue lens to her right eye had slipped to the side, revealing a dark iris beneath.

"You have children here?" Kelly asked in total bewilderment.

"Children? God forbid!" Morris laughed out loud for the first time. "My dear, we keep young goats in the stables under the house, that's all."

He tapped a brogue on the patio. "Right beneath us. They need a lot of feeding, though, I can tell you – especially in the last two weeks. That's the critical period. If you get that wrong, it ruins the taste completely."

I looked across the neatly mown lawn, where Joseph was crouching to inspect the lobster cage in the dying light. But I knew now, of course, that the cage was not designed for a lobster, but for a baby goat. I saw that it would be impossible for a small animal to move within in its tight wicker confines. At the top, the small gap would provide just enough space for the goat's head to stick out for feeding.

"So you're telling me," Kelly said quietly, "that you keep baby goats under this house, in cages, and that you force feed them to make pâté?"

"It isn't *just* pâté. And I can tell you now, my dear, most emphatically, that none of my subjects experience any pain whatsoever."

"How can you possibly know that?"

"Local anaesthetic is administered to ensure that the subjects feel nothing during the fattening process and that the trachea remains numb throughout all feeding sessions. It is such a shame that you insist on being so narrow minded. What difference can it possibly make from an ethical perspective whether it's a duck or a goose or, indeed, a goat?"

I thought of the photograph in the toilet, of the monkey cages and Morris' clean white lab coat. I could still taste the faint iron-like tang of the foie gras. I simply could not speak. In the end, I didn't have to.

Kelly stepped forward and calmly rested her wine glass on the table.

"Mr. Westhoff, I am sorry, but I believe what you are doing here is immoral, despicable and, I suspect, illegal. I thank you for your hospitality but we are leaving now."

Morris only smiled and nodded. "As you wish."

The silence was broken again, not by thunder this time, but by a terrible and prolonged gargling sound that echoed up from beneath us, from deep within the bowels of the Westhoff house.

On the brisk walk back to our farmhouse, the rain finally began to fall. Darkness gathered with our every step. Joseph ran on ahead.

"I meant exactly what I said," Kelly whispered. "We're leaving. Now."

"But the Ferry isn't booked until Friday."

"Change it. Please."

"What will we tell Joseph?"

"Nothing. Put him to bed as usual. We'll put him in the car after he's asleep. When he wakes up, we'll be in Cherbourg."

She was trying to be strong, but I knew her better than that. I could hear the slight tremble in her voice that told me she was not angry, but frightened.

We walked in silence as the ruined cemetery came into view through the rain. It suddenly struck me then.

"Do you think they bury them in the −"

"Yes."

It didn't take long to pack up. I backed the car right up to the house; out of sight from the Westhoff residence, so that no one could know. I was surprised at how in agreement I was with Kelly about leaving tonight. I had felt it too. It wasn't just an argument about food, but something else beneath that. A sense that something was out of kilter here − something was not right with the Westhoffs − and it sent a chill through me. I no longer felt safe for any of us. The edge I had heard in Kelly's voice was all the more unsettling, because I seldom saw her shaken in this way.

Once the car was crammed full, I put my waterproof coat on and pulled the hood over my head.

I made my way down the driveway for one last cigarette before the journey began. Darkness had fallen. The street lamp at the entrance shone light through the beating rain.

I stopped short of the entrance to the driveway when a rustling noise sounded through the rain from just behind the wall of the driveway. I peered through the rain drops, but saw nothing. Was it possible that someone was hidden behind the wall? It would have to be someone small – very small. Someone like Morris.

I stood frozen for a moment, feeling my heart thump wildly under my coat. I had definitely heard something there. I threw my cigarette down and ran back to the house.

I told Kelly we were ready to go and went to Joseph's room to lift him into the car. I walked in and turned on the lights to find his bed empty and his sheets a swirling mess about the floor. Panic took hold almost immediately. I searched each room methodically, even the games room which was a separate out–building from the main house. Nothing.

"Joseph! Joseph!"

I scraped my fingers down my face, as though it may bring rationality of thought. Kelly rushed at me with tears in her eyes.

"Where is he?"

Then it came to me. There was one place I hadn't looked: the bathroom off the main living area. We had barely used it because it was smaller and less clean than the other one between the bedrooms. I pushed the door open and saw the light was already on: a bare bulb dangling from the ceiling.

Joseph was standing absolutely still beside the toilet, a terrified expression stretched across his pale face. He looked at me desperately, and then moved his eyes towards the closed bath curtain beside him, and nodded slowly. I reached out my hand to him and he took it before running out of the bathroom to Kelly, screaming at the top of his lungs.

The bath curtain hung before me, straight and absolutely still.

I stood motionless for some time until my breathing had levelled to quietness. The panic had left me now, although my heart still thumped in my chest like a caged animal. Then I saw the thin white fabric twitch, just once, and realized that Joseph had been right. There was something behind there. I reached out and ripped the curtain back.

Inside the dry bath, a thick brown snake curled and writhed in anger, striking out powerfully at the curtain. I stumbled backwards and ran.

Within minutes, the house was locked with keys safely hidden amongst the flowers by the ornamental cart-wheel. The engine started and I locked the car from the inside before turning on the wipers and heading out into the rain. In the backseat, Joseph was whimpering. Kelly was silent next to me.

I reached the end of the driveway and turned right.

"This isn't the way we came."

"The sat nav's broken," I said. "But forget that. I've checked the map. This is quickest route to the motorway."

As the headlights beamed through the rain, the ruined chapel of Le Carde came into view. A small figure rose from the gravestones in the cemetery and stared back at us through the rain. Pale-faced and dressed in a trenchcoat, he held a spade in one hand.

"Jesus Christ, it's Morris."

"Just keep driving, Tom. For God's sake, keep driving."

And I did – and soon we were on open road, driving through remote French countryside. Every now and then I checked the rear view mirror to make sure we were not being followed. I remembered what Judith had said about the rain: *". . . I so hope it does. It's been twenty-three days now."*

"It's impossible to dig soil when it's that dry," I said aloud. "And twenty-three days is a long time to have to wait to bury something."

By why go to all the trouble? I thought as I squinted into the darkness. *Why bother burying goats? Why not burn them, or simply dump them?*

In the backseat, Joseph was snoring quietly and had wrapped a colourful duvet around himself. Kelly was quiet too, breathing regularly with her head rested against the window. We were still some distance from the motorway and would need to drive through at least three small villages before we reached the safety of the toll gates and the main highway beyond.

I slowed as the road narrowed and gave way to a collection of small houses. This was Saint-Médard, the first of the villages. Though the roads were empty, I was forced to stop at a traffic light. A small white flyer was fastened to its post.

It was the picture of a dark haired toddler. He was missing. This was a call for help. There was a police contact number at the bottom of the picture.

A few yards later, I stopped again at a deserted roundabout. Someone had fastened another flyer to a pillar beside the road. A different child this time; a girl of around four with pale features and curling blonde locks.

Dread crept through me in the coming miles, because as we left Saint-Médard and made our way through more country lanes to the village of L'Isle-de-Noé, it was the same story all over again: photographs of missing children in darkened shop windows, taped roughly to lamp posts and across stone bollards by the roadside.

"That's six now," Kelly said into the silence.

My heart sank then because I thought she was asleep, and I had not wanted her to see what I had seen. But more than that, I could not face discussing the possibilities that now filled my thoughts.

I tried to speak, but no sound came. All I could think about was the lobster cage on the Westhoff's perfectly mown lawn, the photograph of Morris in the toilet, smiling proudly in his white lab coat, the terrible gargling noise that had risen up from beneath the patio, local anaesthetic, and – worst of all – the faint iron-like taste that still lingered on the edges of my tongue.

The Other One

March 1953

Wickfield

Here is my account, as promised. I am sorry it has taken so long but bringing it all to the fore once again has been difficult, as I am sure you understand. In any case, it is done now and I only ask that you keep this safely with the other documents, so there can be a record, so that others may know. Whilst this is not a legal matter – far from it – there is an affliction amongst us solicitors to insist on consigning events to the page and so here is my testimony, for the archives.

I remember everything perfectly of course, much as I have prayed to forget.

The passing months have spared no detail from recollection, allowed no leave from the long shadows cast by Mortimer Lodge. Even in sleep, there is no peace. We have tried to sell the place but that is virtually impossible given the circumstances. It is too soon, as I'm sure you will agree. Still, perhaps it is better that way. I would not wish a similar experience on any living person.

We live many miles from Morton now and though our accommodation is simple, we are content enough each day just to be away from it all.

It began on twenty-second of December last year, although in reality it started long before that. How little I knew.

It was to be our first Christmas at the house. Daniel

had turned five that summer and, just after we moved in, I had secured the Partnership at Elliot Thorpe in Oxford. We loved the house, the village, the quiet country life with its reassuring sense of safety and comfort. Who would not?

It came that morning, hesitantly at first, no more than a handful of lonely flakes dancing against frozen skies. But soon, as the air grew still, the snow began dropping like weighted feathers, settling over the village and surrounding fields in a thick, flawless coating. By lunchtime, three inches were down and Mortimer Lodge, with its ivy-clad Georgian facades and high windows, shadowed by St Anselm's steeple at the rear, was the scene from a Christmas card; complete with snow-layered holly and playful robins, fluttering from the churchyard to our garden.

Daniel's face was a picture as he gazed up at the heavens from the warmth of the living room, his keen blue eyes alive with childish excitement.

Kathleen and I watched him without speaking, cherishing the pure innocence and enthusiasm that only exists in the young at Christmas. Outside, light was fading fast. The clear, unfaltering voices of children practicing carols in St Anselm's permeated the silence. I remember the quality of the sound even now; the haunting notes holding impossibly in the stillness.

In that moment it was as though the complicated puzzle of our lives had suddenly become solved. We had reached a utopia of some kind, surely. But did I feel it, even then? Yes, I think so, that vague sense of unease, of the unknown that lay ahead. Through all the happiness, the contentment, the twinkling of lights and scent of burning logs in the hearth, there lay something beneath, something indefinable and insubstantial but real nonetheless. The holiday was upon us, snow was falling, Christmas was coming but – though I could not yet identify its true nature – so too, was something else.

I woke suddenly in the early hours of twenty-third of December, certain that a loud noise had sounded outside the house. Kathleen lay asleep beside me, her regular breaths whispering through the silence. I crept out of bed and padded to the window.

Outside, Morton was as still as a tomb, its lantern-lit high street now indivisible from the pavement as snow continued to fall like pale ashes. There was to be a Christmas market in the morning and empty scaffold structures had been erected at regular intervals along its length in readiness. A small fox stole in and out of the metal poles before disappearing down a narrow alleyway.

And then I saw him, at the very edge of Moreton, where stone cottages finally give way to open fields. A small boy, standing motionless in the pool of orangey light beneath a street lamp, his face no more than a featureless mask staring back at me from afar. It was difficult to make out but I was certain that his right arm, bent at the elbow, was stuck out in front of his chest, as though paralysed in some way.

The bell at St Anselm's struck the hour, its solemn tone carrying across the fields. I looked at my watch: 3.00am. Insanity for a child to be out at this time, in this weather.

I squinted through the flakes again, towards the

street lamp. This time there was nothing, only the snow steadily falling and the village, utterly still and empty of life. Impossible.

I hurried downstairs, wrapped a coat around myself and pulled my boots on.

I trudged through the garden, past the gate and down the high street, kicking up snow like powder as I passed the empty market stalls and finally reached the street lamp where the boy had stood.

It took me only a moment to realise that there were no tracks beneath the light, only clean, virgin snow glistening in the amber light, inches thick. Impossible – again.

When I eventually emerged the following morning, I found Kathleen and Daniel clearing breakfast away in the kitchen.

"You went out, didn't you," she said, drying her slender hands on a tea towel, "late last night? Your boots are soaking."

"I couldn't sleep. Just needed some air, that's all. "Now," I clapped my hands together, smiling at them both. "Let's see about that market shall we?"

What was I supposed to say? That I had seen a child that did not exist? That I had seen a ghost?

Our arrival at Morton some six months earlier had elicited an agreeable response from the villagers. The house, larger than others in the vicinity and set aside from the main high street, had remained uninhabited for some years prior to our purchase and we were welcomed into the community with no hint of jealousy or grievance. Pressures of work had meant that I had missed the annual summer fete and so I was glad to able to attend the Christmas market all the more because of it.

With thoughts of the previous night fading away with every bright smile from Daniel and Kathleen, we set off into the village.

We strolled leisurely through the market, weaving slowly in and out of the stalls and occasionally stopping to talk to neighbours and newly found friends. It was lovely to watch Kathleen's enthusiasm, so adept at socialisation and finding common ground as she was. Her dark hair shone against the snow and even though her face was half-covered by a woollen scarf, I had forgotten how much her beauty touched me, a stark reminder of how little time I had allocated to her for the sake of The Practice in recent months.

"I'm sorry," I said, squeezing her gloved hand, "I've hardly seen you at all lately. I'll make it up to you."

"You already have," she replied, catching me with emerald eyes, "just by being here. I've not been feeling myself the last few days. I'm really glad you're with us."

"You're unwell?"

"No, I don't mean like that. It's nothing, really. Now, stop being so soppy and bring me mulled wine, immediately."

I had seen the gluvine stall, further back on the opposite side of the street as we had passed, and so I left them both in search of it again.

The air was crisp and frozen, but rich with the shrill laughter of children, brass trumpets and the smell of freshly grilled sausages and candy floss. I slipped through the crowds and trod carefully across the snow-packed road to the other side. As I did so, a voice called out behind me.

"Go easy there, Tom. Terribly icy under foot."

I turned to see Fr Edward before me, smiling broadly with an outstretched hand. He wore an oversized blue anorak with a thick fur collar that made him appear even smaller than he was.

"Icy indeed," I replied, shaking his hand. "Good to see you, Father."

He kept my hand in a vice-like grip whilst asking after Kathleen and Daniel.

"They're very well. They are actually around here somewhere. I'm getting some mulled wine. Can I tempt you?"

"And the house?" he went on, ignoring the question as he clasped his free hand tightly over the top of mine, "everything is good with the house, yes?"

"Well yes, of course." I smiled at him oddly.

"Good, good. So glad to hear it." His little face looked more red than usual, no doubt due to the cold. He scanned the crowd around us, as though searching for something, before finally releasing his grip. "Right, I must catch up with the Jeffersons. I'll maybe see you Christmas Eve then? Early evening mass, yes?"

"Wouldn't miss it for the world."

Soon afterwards he disappeared into the crowd and I stood for a moment, pondering the conversation, trying to make sense of it. I knew nothing then, did I? Not like you Wickfield. You would have known exactly why he was asking about the house.

The most impressive feature of Mortimer Lodge is

without doubt the grand fireplace in the drawing room. Its lime stone masonry runs practically the entire length of the room. There is no need for a guard as the hearth is set so far within the thickness of the eastern wall that one could walk beneath the entire structure should the temptation ever arise.

Later in the day, the market now a fading memory, Kathleen made hot chocolates whilst Daniel and I piled up logs and watched flames grow and lick around blackened stone. The light had dimmed outside and the Christmas tree twinkled in the corner of the room. Kathleen brought the drinks through and we snuggled together on the settee and listened to the wireless as the fire crackled and spat beside us. Every now and then, Daniel padded across the oak flooring and knelt beneath the tree, rearranging various presents into neat little piles, before returning once again to the warmth of the fire.

Less than an hour later, with Kathleen and Daniel fast asleep beside me, I began to feel strangely anxious and unsettled, as though there were something I had forgotten or lost but couldn't quite remember what it was, or had been. I should have been looking forward to Christmas, the three of us together, but all the while something was blocking the light, just out of view, vague and unformed but as real as Kathleen and Daniel's gentle breaths as they slept. Something was wrong, or was about to be.

Beyond the tall windows of the drawing room, light was fading fast; my final opportunity to take a stroll around the village to clear my mind before dusk.

I took the western path to the rear of Mortimer

Lodge, heading towards St Anselm's. Whilst the snow had stopped, the air was bitter and an icy wind pushed against my face, bringing tears to my eyes. On the main track, snow had compacted underfoot, making it difficult to traverse, especially nearing the church, where footfall had trampled the snow into a hard, glistening plate of ice. I used the dry-stone walling for support as I neared the church gates and finally stepped onto frozen grass.

Before me, snow-clad crucifixes and crumbling headstones twisted up from the ground, some adorned with festive wreaths from those wishing loved ones glad tidings, even in death. A crow cawed into the silence and, as I turned, I glimpsed movement at the far end of the graveyard, in the shadows of a large yew tree.

I squinted into the dying light. Yes, there it was again. I could see him now, in between the dark branches, half hidden from sight. A man, very tall, dressed in black. Incredibly thin. Pale, drawn features. Despite the warmth of my coat, a shiver ran down my spine as I moved towards the tree.

"Hello?" I called. "Who's there?"

But as I crunched through the snow, meandering through the graves and half-buried crosses to the shadow of the yew, I saw that I had been mistaken. There was nothing, only a small robin perched on a branch, twitching its head this way and that, chirping into the silence, only the dank smell of yew resin and old earth.

I looked to the frozen ground, where a crumbling headstone protruded from the soil, the very spot where I had seen the man. It was the only headstone in the vicinity, as though it had been intentionally set aside from all the other graves.

I crouched and brushed away the snow to reveal the worn lettering beneath:

Terrence Mortimer
1 November 1832 – 26 July 1888

"Mortimer," I whispered, wondering if there was some connection with Mortimer Lodge.

But it was unlikely. The house was Georgian – built in 1745 – eighty-seven years before Terrence Mortimer's birth.

I was awoken that night, just before midnight, once again with the notion that a noise nearby had stirred me. Hesitantly, I moved to the window and peeled back the curtain.

The boy was there again, not in the village as before but on the lawn this time, beside the spidery branches of the willow at the far eastern corner. His silhouette was absolutely still against the whiteness as he stared up at the house. Though it was too shadowed to make out his pale features, I saw once again that his arm was held out before him, bent at the elbow. A polished surface glinted in the moonlight. I could see now: not a real arm, but a wooden prosthetic, strapped with old leather at the elbow.

A large bird of prey glided across the lawn, distracting me momentarily. When I looked again, the boy was gone.

Soon afterwards I fell into a deep slumber, as

though the incident had drained all energy from me. My dreams were haunted with images of the boy, not motionless anymore but striding through the snow intently, towards the house, arm protruding. I was aware of banging noises, of a terrible scraping sound, like rough bricks grating against one another. Then another noise, a piercing scream that echoed about Mortimer Lodge, waking me with a start. Daniel.

"I'll go," I told Kathleen, leaping from the sweat-drenched covers and racing across the darkened landing to his room. I hit the light switch to find him sitting bolt upright in bed, shrieking hysterically.

"It's all right," I said, holding his warm body next to mine, rocking him until his tense little muscles relaxed. "You had a bad dream that's all. Don't worry. Hush now."

"Wasn't a dream, Daddy."

"It's all right.'

"It was knocking at the door," he snivelled, "I thought it was Santa."

"Santa's not until tomorrow," I said gently.

"I thought he was early and couldn't get down the chimney. It wasn't Santa though. It was a boy. He had a funny arm."

A cold chill ran through me.

"I couldn't stop him coming in and now he's downstairs. His eyes are wrong." He began to whimper into the silence again. "I'm sorry, Daddy. I didn't mean to."

"Just a bad dream," I repeated quietly. "Just a silly old dream. There's no one there."

Just then, Kathleen entered the room. I smiled as

reassuringly as I could, telling her I'd be through in a moment, and not to worry.

Once Daniel was settled, I switched on the landing lights and went downstairs. The house was absolutely silent – unnaturally so – and I checked each room to find everything as it should be.

Before heading back upstairs, I went to the front door and found one of the kitchen chairs sitting beside it. I knew instantly how it had come to be there. Daniel had stood on it to reach the lock and open the door.

"There's something wrong in this house," Kathleen whispered as I got back into bed. "I've felt it coming for days, and now it's here."

"I've checked the whole place," I said. "There is nothing."

I was trying hard to make sense of it all, to bring some kind of rationality, but the hairs across my back prickled and stood on end as I saw Kathleen's expression across the pillows.

"I'm telling you, Tom, there's something with us, in this house, something dead."

The following morning Daniel remembered nothing. I have heard that children have a way blocking traumatic events from memory. If only it was as simple for us adults.

"Santa's coming tonight, Daddy," he said merrily over his cornflakes.

"Yes, I know." I forced a smile but all I could think of was the little boy with the wooden arm, and the tall figure I had seen at the graveyard. I turned to Kathleen as she entered the kitchen.

"There's something I need to do," I said. "I'll be an

hour or so and then we'll talk properly about all of this. Will you be all right here?"

"Please don't be long."

I found Fr Edward inside St Anselm's, preparing flowers beside the altar on bended knee. Candles flickered and twinkled as I strolled down the aisle toward him. As I approached, he stood and turned to me with an expression of concern.

"Yesterday," I said, hearing my voice echo into the silence, "you asked me if everything was all right with the house. Well, it's not – it's not all right at all."

A short silence followed. Fr Edward sighed into the quietness and bowed his head for a moment, as though deep in prayer.

"I was concerned this may happen," he said at length, turning to face the golden cross that hung above the altar. "He's come back again, hasn't he? The Boy."

"It's happened before?"

It was odd but the revelation both angered and comforted me simultaneously. Angered, because I had been hoodwinked in some way, but comforted by the knowledge that I was not losing my mind after all. But then something else too, beneath that, more profound, a realisation that the dead really could return and walk amongst the living.

"Sometimes at Christmas he's been seen in the village and outside Mortimer Lodge. As you know, the house was empty for some time before you bought it. I was hoping your arrival may have broken the spell, so to speak."

"Who is he?" I said. "And who is the other one, the

tall man?"

Fr Edward turned to me. Something different clung to his expression now: no longer simply concern, but fear. He lifted his ashen face with narrowed eyes.

"Where did you see the other one?"

"Here," I said, "at St Anselm's. In the churchyard, by the grave of Terrence Mortimer."

Even as I said the name, I sensed the atmosphere change. It was cold, standing there in the church as we were, but now the temperature seemed to drop further still.

"I think it's important you talk to Wickfield," he said nervously, eyeing the space the around us. "He will tell you everything you need to know. He's working today. Follow me."

At that point, of course, I had no idea who you were Wickfield, and was wholly expecting to be led outside into the snow, perhaps to your house or to your place of work in the village. Instead, Fr Edward walked ahead of me, through the heavy wooden doorway in the vestry and down the spiralling stone steps to the crypt. Except that 'crypt' is not the right word is it, Wickfield? More a library, a chained library.

Quite a sight too, with its ancient leather volumes, stretching from floor to vaulted stone, each shackled through the spine by weighty chains that look as old as the books themselves. When I first saw you, you were hunched over a hand-written manuscript at the reading desk, beneath a small lamp, magnifying glass in hand. The studious librarian. The keeper of history, and of secrets. How many years have you tended that place?

Fr Edward stepped forward from the darkness.

"Wickfield, this is Tom. As you probably know, he and his family bought the Mortimer house earlier this year. All's been well until now but lately, they've been having a few issues. The boy has returned. And also . . . the other one. I was wondering if you might be kind enough to show Tom the history. So that he can understand."

I will not narrate the fine detail of all you recounted in the dim light of the chained library that morning. There would be little point in that. Anyone reading this will simply view the documents beneath, the ones that you showed me.

What is there to tell? On Christmas Eve in 1887, eight year old Joshua Mortimer disappeared from Mortimer Lodge, the family home for many generations, where he resided with his father, Terrence Mortimer, a successful antiques dealer.

Joshua was never seen alive again. Rumours were widespread that Terrence – infamous for his temper – had murdered the child in a drunken rage but the body was never found, despite numerous Police searches. It was believed that Terrence despised the child as his wife, Victoria, had died during the birth and that Joshua had arrived in this world – in Terrence's view – incomplete, with only one arm below the elbow.

In July of the following year, Terrence was found hanging from a yew tree in the churchyard at St Anselm's, wearing his best suit. This only perpetuated speculation that he had killed Joshua and was eventually haunted to insanity by his own actions. The villagers buried him aside from the other graves to mark their beliefs.

A terrible story, of course, but it is the old photograph that stays with me the most. Up until then I could have conceived that everything I had seen had been imagined but now, in seeing it, I knew there could be no doubt.

Joshua and Terrence sit beside the fireplace in the sitting room at Mortimer Lodge. Nothing of any real significance has changed in the room itself to this day. A thin smile plays around Terrence's lips and his upright composure and clenched fist about walking stick provide a sense of brooding menace. One eyebrow slightly cocked, his dark eyes stare intently at the camera. Joshua is expressionless and pale. His eyes tell a different story. His wooden arm protrudes before him, strapped and bound, just as I had witnessed on the lawn the previous night.

"Why does the boy comes back?" I asked Fr Edward.

"There are many reasons why the dead return. Some are here because they are trapped and cannot move on. Others bear a grudge and will not rest until a wrong has been righted. Perhaps Joshua just wants to be at home for Christmas – the Christmas he never had. It is impossible to know with any certainty. In any case, Tom, the boy is only seen on the lead-up to Christmas. When it is done, he will be gone again. And so will the other one too. Take heart in that, if nothing else."

"So there is nothing to be done then."

"I can bless the house, by all means, but it may stir things up. My gut feeling is that we wait. This time tomorrow it will all be over."

Back at the house, whilst Daniel sat drawing with crayons at the kitchen table, I took Kathleen aside and told her everything. She listened without speaking, occasionally rubbing her arms to keep the chill away.

When I was finished she turned her gaze to the crackling fire and asked, "And do you think he's right, that it will all end tomorrow?"

"It makes sense. It's what's happened every year until now."

A burning log hissed into the silence before popping like a cracker around the hearth.

"Do you think we found this place by chance, or something else?" she said.

"What do you mean?"

"You know what I mean, Tom. You said the house had been in the Mortimer family for many generations."

"It's coincidence," I replied. "Nothing more."

But deep in my heart I knew that she may have uncovered something. Until now I had thought nothing of it. Kathleen's mother's maiden name had also been Mortimer.

We spent the rest of the afternoon cleaning the house in preparation for the big day. Daniel and I loaded logs from the shed into a wheel barrow and brought them across the icy driveway to house. Later, whilst he was busy making a snowman on the lawn, Kathleen and I sorted through the stocking presents and made sure everything was in order.

We tried our best to keep busy, to distract ourselves from all that had happened, but it was impossible to ignore the tension that was steadily building in Mortimer Lodge, laden with keen anticipation. Each hour that passed left a deeper, more watchful silence in its wake.

I'm not sure how we would have coped on our own but Daniel's excitement was tangible and overriding. He simply could not wait.

At six o'clock, a hard knock at the front door broke the quietness. Kathleen and I exchanged a nervous glance and Daniel jumped up from the Christmas tree to follow me to the hallway.

I opened the door to a large congregation of carol singers. One held up a Victorian oil lamp, casting an orangey glow across their young faces as they began to sing *Silent Night*. For a moment, I thought I glimpsed the boy at the back of the group, half in obscurity, eyes shadowed against pale features but, as I strained to see more clearly, he was gone again, lost into darkness.

Shortly afterwards, the Christmas bells of St Anselm's began ringing across the village, signalling the imminent commencement of early evening mass. We wrapped ourselves in coats and scarves and gloves and made our way, hand-in-hand, along the western path behind the house, through the snowy graveyard and into the church.

Once through the excited bustle of families crowding the aisle, we found a space on a darkened pew beside the thick granite column that separates the belly of the church from the south transept. Decorations adorned every crevice: holly wreaths bound in red ribbon, glittering tinsel, snow-spayed fir cones and tea candles twinkling into the dimness. I laid our coats and scarves on the empty space beside us and peered down the aisle to see our old friends from Oxford, Colin and Margaret Bull, take a seat a few pews behind. We waved and smiled at one another before the organ blasted into the silence and we stood for the first carol. Daniel was silent throughout the entire service, transfixed by the spectacle and atmosphere of ritual and good will, incense and choir music.

Afterwards, outside, Colin and Margaret Bull greeted us with handshakes and kisses for Daniel and Kathleen. It was so good to see them. They were not from the village and had only come out to Morton to visit other friends living locally. I could see that Kathleen felt the same way too. Her smile was radiant once again, but it melted away just as quickly.

"Who was the other boy with you?" asked Colin.

"Who do you mean?" Kathleen said.

"Well, the one sitting next to you in church, of course. The one with the bad arm."

"Oh, he belongs to someone else," I broke in. "He isn't with us."

As we huddled together and made our way back to the house, our shadows stretched out before us in the snow like elongated insects.

"He *is* with us though," Kathleen said quietly. "There's no question of that."

And now, as I gazed on at our shadows once again, I saw another spindly form, drifting beside ours; faint and insubstantial, almost to the point of translucency, but there just the same, stretching out beside ours as the lights of Mortimer Lodge came into view.

In the sitting room, the fire had burnt down to a heap of glowing embers and pale ashes. I poured a neat whisky and gulped it down in an attempt to numb my nerves. The house felt wrong. I knew it the moment we had set foot through the door. It was as though someone was here with us, watching our every move intently. A hissing silence filled every room, building again as the minutes passed. I poured another and knocked it back again.

The door creaked open and Daniel entered, bearing milk and a plate of mince pies to place beneath the chimney. I smiled and kissed and hugged him good night.

"Santa's coming," he whispered, putting a finger to his lips. "It's nearly time."

And so it began.

Kathleen woke me just before midnight, shaking and hitting me into sobriety.

"Wake up, Tom. For God's sake, wake up!"

"What?"I was annoyed and heavy headed. "What's the matter?"

"Listen."

I sat upright and listened into the silence. At first there was nothing, but then it came. A heavy grating noise, the one I had heard in my dreams, like rough bricks being rubbed across one another from somewhere downstairs, below our room.

"I'll take a look. Pass me the torch."

"I'm coming with you."

Together we crept down the stairs like frightened children, towards the origin of the noise which grew louder and louder as we approached the sitting room.

I pushed the door open and switched on the lights. Now there was only silence. The fire had long since burnt out and apart from the fairy lights on the Christmas tree, twinkling intermittent, the room was absolutely still.

But then it came again, the grating sound.

"It's coming from the fireplace," Kathleen said.

As the grating continued, I moved toward the hearth and switched on the torch. I realised, as I approached, that the sound was coming from above, up inside the chimney itself. I stepped around the mince pies and milk and crouched beneath it, shining the light upwards.

"It must be an animal." I said, tracking the beam around the inside of the chimney. "It's trapped in the brickwork up there. But I can't see it."

I reached up to the area where the noise was coming from. My fingers passed over rough bricks and I felt the vibration of the sound through them. I pulled at a loose one. It fell immediately on to my shoulder, causing me to cry out in pain.

"Tom, get out of there, before the whole thing collapses."

I stumbled away from the fireplace as more bricks fell from above, clunking around the hearth and echoing into the night.

Then something else fell in a great heap, smashing the glass of milk and covering the mince pies.

Behind me Kathleen gasped. I turned to see her covering her mouth with her hand, eyes wide in terror.

When I looked to the fireplace, I saw now what had fallen: yellowed, splintered bones, a gaping skull, a small wooden prosthetic arm. Joshua.

The sound of Daniel thumping down the stairs broke through the quietness.

"Daddy! It's Santa. He's coming down the chimney."

"Don't let him in here," I ordered.

Kathleen staggered backwards to lean against the door.

In that moment I became aware of another presence in the room. A dark and unyielding force, filled with malice and ill intent.

"We've got to get out of here," whispered Kathleen. "There's something terrible here."

"Daddy, let me in. I want Santa."

And as I turned to the door, I saw the other one, towering over the Christmas tree beside the window. Tall, malevolent and filled with rage at our discovery.

Kathleen staggered forwards in helpless fear. Daniel burst into the room and screamed as he saw the bones in the fireplace and Terrence Mortimer behind the tree.

"He's not real," I shouted. "Don't worry, Daniel, he's not real. Look away!"

And then all was silent. It was over.

You know the rest, Wickfield. The police enquiry and all that followed. The final chapter of the history: the murder of Joshua Mortimer at the hands of his father, Terrence, finally proven beyond doubt.

I have been back to the house, more than once, to collect our belongings, but I never stay long. Terrence is always there. He bears a grudge and will not leave. We have exposed him and there are scores to settle.

As for Kathleen's family connection to the Mortimers, I will leave that for you to research, Wickfield. You are more practised in these matters than I.

Yours sincerely

Tom Redfern

The Setting Sea

If you are reading this letter then I have succeeded in recording my fate and you now walk in my footsteps. I wish you well, although it will do you little good. Perhaps though, in providing you with certainty of outcome, I will impart the resolve you will most certainly require.

Finding a diamond in amongst the rubble doesn't happen very often but when it does, it justifies all the futile searches that have gone before. But to identify a diamond you must first be able to distinguish it from quartz; must understand the structure of cuts that define it as being exquisite or simply average. And it is the same with art, to a point, because to find a painting of value, you must first know intimately the history of the artist in question. Circles, squares and two-dimensional faces painted roughly on canvas could be just that to one viewer but, to the discerning, could give proof of a rare Pintero. My expertise lies in oils – always has – and after thirty-three years in the business, I know my field.

To have any chance of finding the elusive diamond you must first go to the quarries. In my case, this means attending car boot sales in remote locations and contents-auctions of the recently deceased. You can find what you want at the auction houses but more often than not a painting will sell for its market worth, which completely defeats the object. After all, how can I turn a profit when I have paid the full price? Where's my margin? And sitting on paintings in the hope of value increases in future years is simply not my game. No matter how dirty I get, I know the quarries hold the profit I seek and that all I need do, is keep on digging.

I had been one of the first to arrive at the barely advertised gathering at Cross Hill Farm. I had parked and wandered across the muddy ground to the sellers' area to begin my usual inspection of the stalls.

To start with, I saw nothing but the predictable clutter: crass china ornaments, half-complete tool kits, dated 35mm film cameras and various collections of mismatched books, tattered woollen clothing and vinyl records. The only framed pictures I found were the clichéd imprints of chocolate-box thatched cottages set against spring flowers and faux Parisian scenes of white flowing dresses and swirling parasols. Joy.

Then I saw it. A flat, square object wrapped in white cloth, sandwiched between a world atlas and a tarnished mirror.

I knelt down on the wet grass, reached under the table and raised it to the light.

The moment I unravelled the canvas from its ragged bedding and viewed the unframed painting for the first time, I knew I had found my diamond.

It was a Yeats. Of that, there could be absolutely no doubt.

The combination of dark, theatrical skies hanging above the ocean's imposing swell – all textured in delicate lashes by the finest weasel-hair brush – was proof enough for me. Even the abandoned lighthouse itself, contrasting perfectly against the ominous skies, was painted with such skill and detail that the tide marks around its base possessed an almost photographic quality.

But it was the slim figure of the hanging man,

dangling on a noose from the grimy railings of the lighthouse's balcony that was the classic hallmark of Yeats; the familiar, morbid subject matter that had set him apart – estranged him even – from his peers at the turn of the century.

I scanned the base of the painting for the signature that I hoped would not be there. Yeats only ever signed his pictures on the reverse of the canvas.

There was no signature and so I shakily turned it over and sure enough, inked in neat hand at the bottom left-hand corner of the yellowed material, was the name, *Edward Yeats*. And then beneath that, the words, *Barons Point*.

In all my years I had never seen a textbook replication of this work, or even heard mention of it, and yet I was certain of its authenticity. It was that rarest of finds: the undiscovered original.

I rose to my feet to address the seller, an elderly man dressed in beige chinos and pinstripe shirt. From beneath his straw boater he grinned to expose jagged, rotten teeth against bronzed skin.

"How much do you want for this one?" I asked evenly.

"It's yours for five pounds."

I studied the picture for long seconds, feigning indecision.

I had been here many times before. It was a delicate balance. To give an immediate affirmation would risk revealing to the seller the painting's significant worth, but to overplay the indecision act could have the same effect.

In the end, and given the lack of rival punters in the

field, I used the well-rehearsed technique that had served so well over the years, and put the painting down on the table between us.

"It's a bit much," I said, "but thanks anyway."

I turned and began strolling away.

"I'll give it to you for four pounds," he called after me – as I knew he would – and it was difficult not to laugh then, with knowledge of the picture's true value.

I stretched out my careful consideration of the painting for a moment longer, before finally agreeing.

"Much obliged," he said as I passed over the money.

"No," I replied. "Thank you."

He fixed me with keen blue eyes that twitched a little as he smiled.

To narrow any chance of invalidation of the sale, I returned to the car immediately, only looking back once I was inside with the engine running and the picture resting safely on the passenger seat beside me. The old man was nowhere to be seen among the stalls and tabletops. I checked the rear-view mirror, thinking that perhaps he was making his way to me, in sudden realisation. Nothing.

I needn't have worried. Minutes later, with the road stretching ahead of me and not a car in sight, I shrieked with delight at the fortune fate had served me. The Yeats, if independently verified as original – which I knew it would be – would easily fetch a high, five-figure sum. Not a bad profit turn on a four-pound purchase.

A small pang of guilt momentarily threatened to cloud my elation. How could I take advantage of an old man's naivety? How could I justify the immorality of the transaction that I had designed so deceitfully? But then, of course, I remembered that this was business and that margins were the key. Getting dirty in the quarry was all part of coming out on top, and that's exactly what I had done, regardless of an old man's incompetence.

On the way back to the house, passing mile upon mile of dreary, sodden landscape, my mind wandered to the ultimate objective: the villa in Tuscany. So close now. I could almost smell the grapes from the lined vineyards that stretched through the sunlit valleys. Was it possible that this final nugget would facilitate the dream and that I would reach the final destination after all this time? Yes.

And forget morality.

"Thank God for stupid old bastards," I said into the quietness.

With no spouse or offspring, I was free to do as I pleased and until now money had been my only obstacle. But if I could just realise the correct price for the Yeats then it wouldn't be long before I was bathing in golden Tuscan dreams. Bliss.

Back at the house I mounted the picture in a conventional wooden frame and hung it, as was my custom, on the wall in the attic room where illumination from the skylight window was perfect and even.

Now I could see clearly how Yeats had created drama in the picture.

A large cloud, thickly painted in dark blue hues, but lined with bright yellow edges, obscured the sun. From its gleaming perimeter, beams of sunlight poured onto the sea at various depths; one to the foreground, one to the mid then another, smaller ray to the ocean in the background, creating an extraordinary sense of depth. At each depth, tiny brush strokes had been used to create a glistening effect on the surface of the dark ocean, like thousands of wriggling fish.

In the foreground – where grassy dunes gave way to pure sand – a small black dog sat, back-facing the viewer but with its nose pointing far above to the lighthouse, and the hanging man – a perfect compositional technique that drew the viewer's eye from one corner of the image to the other.

Looking now in detail at the figure of the hanging man, I saw that his torso was naked and that his thin arms fell limply to his sides with his head dangling to his chest, obscuring features. It was macabre but fascinating too. Yeats had had a talent for combining the beautiful and the hideous to create not just a picture but a story too, or rather a snap shot of a story, within which the viewer would have to create a beginning and an end.

But there was something wrong.

On closer inspection it was apparent that the image of the hanging man did not possess the same intricate brushwork and detail as the rest of the painting. Here the strokes were thicker and less defined, as though the base layers of oil had been applied but not the final coating. Why had Yeats not finished it?

As I continued gazing at the image, I had the strangest sensation that someone was standing directly behind me, watching over my shoulder, but when I turned there was nothing, only the floorboards of the attic room and the silence.

Using a magnifying glass, I inspected the quality of the paint across the entire landscape. It was arid and cracked in places but for the most part had stood the test of time. The only real flaw was a triangular mark on the balcony of the lighthouse where a tiny section of paint had cracked and fallen away, exposing the canvas beneath.

But that was an easy fix: no more than a dab of carefully selected colour would conceal it.

Later in the day, I consulted my collection of art history books in an attempt to source mention of the painting that now hung in the attic room. I found nothing, but the more I viewed Yeats's other paintings, the more certain I became that this was an original. All of his works were painted in the same, dramatic style with an element of death. In one picture, known only as *The Mill*, Yeats had painted in stunning detail an old water mill at the edge of a tree-shrouded lake. Among the lilies at the bank lay the lifeless body of a man, face down in the water.

In another, Yeats had painted a seascape – a beach set under heavy skies where a solitary figure sat in a deck chair facing the ocean. One arm hung limply over the rest, just above the sand. Was he sleeping, or was he dead?

The more I read of Yeats, the more interested I became.

Born to a wealthy Berkshire family in 1842 where expectation for his future lay in Oxford to study law, Yeats swam against the tide to make his name in the world of art. His light touch and uncanny ability to create three-dimensional landscapes soon had his contemporaries scratching their heads. Yeats continued to improve and impress throughout the late 1800s, painting scenes around the Dorset coast, until the introduction of the uniquely sinister element to his work.

Shunned by critics and colleagues alike, and despite a lack of sales, Yeats continued on his dark path in the hope that critics would eventually acknowledge and give recognition to the originality of his paintings. It never came.

Broke and laden with resentment that his work would never sell for its true worth, Yeats vowed to seek revenge on his contemporaries and critics, but instead drank himself to an early death in the winter of 1900. As with many artists of the era, his works only found the recognition that he so desperately sought, after his death.

I admired Yeats enormously, not for just for his indisputable talent but also for his refusal to alter his vision to fit a more popular view. He painted what he painted and believed in it unwaveringly. Unrewarded though he was, it was only artists such as Yeats who pushed boundaries. And in my view, boundaries need always be pushed when it comes to art.

It seemed unjust that Yeats had worked all his life without realising his dream, and yet here I was on the verge of realising mine, at least in part because of what he had unknowingly achieved.

I had no idea where Barons Point was but knew that, if it were proved that the lighthouse stood somewhere on the coast of Dorset, it would add weight to the ever-mounting substantiation that this was, indeed, an original Yeats.

I found my map in the boot of the car and spread it across the kitchen table, tracing a finger around Dorset's coastline: Swanage; Lulworth Cove; Durdle Door; Peaker Edge; *Barons Point*.

Though I was more convinced than ever of the painting's authenticity, I knew it would not be proof enough for the rigorous requirements of the open market. I needed independent verification, and knew exactly where to get it.

There are few recognised authorities on Dorset's many artists – both dead and living – but the finest amongst them is David Whieldon, whom I had met intermittently throughout my career at various art exhibitions and auctions. It would be a long drive to Dorset to have him authenticate the painting, but would be worth it. Once he had metaphorically rubber-stamped the work of art as a true Yeats, the sky was the limit and I would be one step closer to Tuscany.

I rang him immediately to arrange a meeting the following day. He obliged, with interest.

"So what exactly do you have?"

"Something extraordinary," I told him, "if I'm right, that is. I'll see you at noon."

I woke early, carefully packed the painting in the boot of the car, and jotted down the directions in my notebook before taking to the open road.

In less than two hours I had reached the remote valley – nestled deep in the heart the Purbecks – where the small settlement of Lultown lay huddled in the silent landscape. Sheep-dotted hills rose steeply to either side and far above, buzzards glided in effortless circles against clear April skies. I passed no one as I strolled through the village to Whieldon's small art outlet at the end of the High Street.

The leaded windows were darkened and a crooked *closed* sign hung at the door. Surely not. I cupped my hands to the glass and peered into the dimness. The place was void of life. I checked my watch: noon, exactly.

I started as a croaky voice sounded behind me. "It's closed."

I turned to see a little old woman before me, stooped and carrying a wicker basket filled with tins of food and fruit. She raised her face and scrutinised me from behind misty blue eyes.

"Yes, I can see that," I replied, hearing faint annoyance in my tone. "I'm here for a meeting with Mr Whieldon."

"You're a friend then."

"I've known David for many years," I said, squinting through the window again. "Yes."

When I turned to her this time, I saw that her expression had softened, the deep wrinkles about her eyes lulling into sadness.

"Well, I'm sorry," she said quietly. "But David passed away last night. There was an accident near Poole. Car accident. Terrible thing to happen. A good man. A good family man was David. You'll know that."

I could hardly believe it, especially after such a long drive to get here. More problems. It was tragic about David – truly - but now I was left with the dilemma of finding another, less-regarded authority to provide the stamp of authenticity that I required for the Yeats painting.

Filled with disappointment, I returned to the car and headed back through the valleys. I had been driving less than ten minutes when I saw the turnstile at the roadside, by the edge of an unfarmed field.

I screeched the car to a halt and reversed back to it, just to make sure I hadn't been mistaken.

Above the turnstile, a battered wooden sign read, *Barons Point.*

I simply couldn't resist taking a look, even if it was just to see if the lighthouse still existed.

I parked and followed the grassy path that led through a small copse before inclining steeply to the brow of rugged hill. From here, the ocean was a grey, shimmering mass on the horizon. The scent of salt hung in the breeze for a moment then was lost again as I followed the path down towards the sea.

Soon the ground levelled and the grass became sparse, giving way to sandy dunes and, as I approached the beach, the lighthouse came into view, rising up from its rocky base like a long-forgotten sentinel, watching silently over the waves.

I stopped then, realising that I now stood in the exact spot where Yeats must have painted his picture all those years ago.

It had barely altered.

The swell of the tide broke gently on the shoreline, its foaming fingers creeping towards me. The tangy smell of seaweed hung in the breeze. Far above, a seagull screamed. I was completely alone here.

I turned to the derelict lighthouse and saw that the door, hanging open from the crumbling tide-marked base, was gently creaking back and forth in the wind.

What would be the harm?

Inside the air was as cold and still and as I ascended the spiral staircase within, the sound of the breaking waves and screeching gulls was swallowed by the echo of my footsteps. Through a battered wooden door at the top step, the circular room at its peak – littered with bird droppings and the shells of long-dead crabs – was completely exposed to the elements.

Salty wind rushed over my face as I stepped over a discarded length of rope and rested my hands on the balcony railings to gaze down at the beach.

Then I saw him, standing on the sand where only moments ago I had stood. He wore the same straw boater hat, pinstripe shirt and chinos that he had done at the car boot sale.

He stared back up at me and raised a hand. In shock, I did the same, knowing that coincidence was an impossibility, and that he must have followed me from Berkshire.

He held up a dark bottle and swayed a little before taking a swig and laughing.

"For four pounds," he called out through the wind. "You can finish it for me."

With that, he turned and made his way back to the dunes.

Unable to move, I watched him disappear among the mounds of grassy sand and, for a reason that I cannot explain, a part of me wanted to shout the word,

"*Yeats*," but there was nothing I could do. I should have been running to catch him, to stop him before he reached the boot of my car, but I was frozen.

As I continued to stare across the landscape, a small black dog came into view, padding slowly up the beach before finally stopping to sit on the sand beneath the lighthouse and gaze up at me.

In that moment a dark cloud passed over the sun, casting shadow across the waters and the beach, but three beams of light rayed down from its golden edges: one near the beach; another in the middle of the darkening sea, and a third near the horizon.

I must have passed out, because when I came around again, I was lying on the balcony, disoriented and struggling for breath. I tried to stand but slipped on the wet grey mess around me.

The pungent scent of linseed oil and turpentine filled my lungs. I gasped frantically for air but finally, gripping the slimy balcony railings for support, I managed to stumble to my feet and take in the scene: waves of gently rolling black sludge, slopping at the shoreline and reaching all the way to the horizon; the dark cloud, unmoving while the rays glistened on the oily surface below; the small dog on the beach, motionless but all-seeing.

I scrambled towards the door that led to the stairwell but as I reached it, my hands merely slipped over its greasy surface to a rough, unyielding texture beneath that I knew all too well: canvas.

Impossible.

Turning, I noticed a triangular patch on the balcony which had been unaffected by the paint. I thought of the painting, of the singular flaw I had found: the triangular chip of paint that had come away, exposing the canvas beneath.

The area was completely dry and inside it lay the length of rope I had previously stepped over. I made my way to it carefully but fell at the last as the fumes overwhelmed me once again.

I dreamt of Italy, of Tuscan hills where vineyards rolled to the horizon, bathed in amber glow. Sunshine warmed my face and I smiled with contentment.

When I woke it was different. The first thing that struck me was the quietness. No more rolling waves or seagulls, just the muffled faraway sound of water sloshing far below a solid surface.

I reached up to my face and felt the thickening crust of paint on skin. Somehow managing to stand, I stared across the ocean, now no more than a solid blue-black mass, slowly hardening beneath the rays of the concealed sun. On the beach, the dog was a two dimensional shape with pale blue paint-dashed eyes.

I reached for the balcony rail and felt across its jagged, brush-stroked surface. I pressed down a little and it gave under the pressure like the icing on a cake that has only partially set.

Overcome with nausea, I fell to my knees, vomiting large clumps of grey sludge onto the balcony's slippery surface. When I had finished, I removed my jacket and top to wipe the drying paint from my hands and face.

Inside my jacket, I found my notebook and pen − this notebook − and decided to recount my fate, as you see it now. I will leave it in the dry triangular space that is unaffected by the changes.

It is different now.

There are other sounds – creaking and ticking sounds that haunt the horizon and echo across the nightmarish landscape to the lighthouse.

The setting has begun in proper. Solidifying is taking its course. A moment ago I touched the brittle, scaly surface of my face. Blinking is becoming almost impossible.

I have a choice: do I simply endure the slow agony of becoming solid and setting to death – or do I use the rope and end it now?

You already know the path I took. You have seen it in the painting you bought. I'll bet you acquired it for a song. I imagine it will be different now though.

The hanging man will be stroked in fine detail, finished at last.

I will leave you to make your own choice.

Alderway

"Swear that you'll never go to the church at Alderway. Swear it."

Your last words to me, Caroline. How they haunt me now.

For years I had assumed they meant nothing and were simply a by-product of the increased morphine dosage in your bloodstream during those final hours. They told me that the drugs would bring you comfort but all I saw was confusion and fear. I shudder to recall the desperate minutes I witnessed your sanity melt into a distorted grimace. You were gone far before your pulse slowed to a stop, and your hand became cold in mine.

"Of course," I said. "I swear it."

Yes, for many years, I thought nothing more of those words and focussed instead on the memories that brought warmth: the way sunlight played across your dark hair in summer time; the tender feel of your lips against mine; the scent of jasmine on your skin. I had never known or even heard of Alderway, or that there should be a church there, until I found your work in the attic.

Having lived alone here for so long, I had assumed that I knew every inch of this house, but I was wrong. The sliding compartment at the bottom of the leather chest was the perfect place – just enough room for the crumpled sheets of paper – the roughly sketched family trees and brass-rubbings. Why did you not destroy it all, Caroline? Why did you not burn everything? But in the end, I cannot blame you. You hid it well enough, and how could you have known you would become ill so suddenly, or that I would ever find it?

I had always harboured an interest in discovering my family history and I could only imagine, as I knelt in the attic with your papers splayed out before me, that – knowing this – you had chosen to find out for yourself, with the intention of surprising me at some future point.

But of course, once you had discovered all there was to discover, you hid it. And who could blame you?

As I unrolled the larger brass-rubbing – the one of the knight's face behind armoured visor – I felt as you must have felt on seeing it that first time: excitement that the similarity was too apparent to be coincidental, and also the distant but unmistakeable sense of dread; the fleeting chill across skin that could not be accounted for.

Do you remember, on summer mornings, how we used to watch fallow deer creep from the woodland and graze on the roses at the far western corner of the lawn? If we so much as flinched from our concealed vantage point in the sitting room, they would twitch their heads and scatter into the trees immediately. I kept a record in the hope of understanding their pattern of behaviours, how often they might visit the lawn and at what times. You mocked me but I would tell you, as always, that everything bears its own unique pattern, that there is always symmetry and regularity; and that you only need look for it. Even now I hold this true. I am retired, but I will always be a mathematician.

It is different now. The deer seldom come to the lawn and when they do, it is not my movements in the sitting room that startle them. They are already anxious because they sense something in the trees about them. They never stay to eat the roses anymore. Their pattern has been knocked out of kilter.

For the longest time, I resisted. But with every year that passed, with every November that dark clouds bloated in the skies above the house and cold rain beat against its windows, I was reminded of your passing; was reminded of your final words and of the secret that would always remain between us, unless I was to visit the church at Alderway and find out for myself whatever it was that lay sheltered there.

It became harder and harder as time went on to ignore that something had been kept from me, but also that I had the power to change it, and that there was no reason why I should not know.

After all, besides breaking my promise to you, what harm could it do?

The journey took less than an hour from the house. So strange that I should never have known of the place; although it is well-hidden. Even on ordinance survey maps no more than a solitary black cross set in open contours with the word *'Alderway'* hanging above it, suggests its existence.

I drove through Compton and into the valley below Pangley, where the road narrowed and became a tunnel of low-hanging branches, clawing around me like skeletal fingers. But soon the landscape opened onto fields again. I passed deserted farmyards, deeply-ploughed fields where crows winged against heavy skies; and all the while, as I drove deeper into remote acreage, the distant sense of dread that I had first experienced grew closer; but I brushed it aside, assuming that my guilt at breaking my promise to you was clouding my reason.

How little I knew.

A mile or so from my destination the road narrowed again. Wild branches scratched intermittently against the side of the car and rain began to fall. There was only room for one vehicle here but I passed no one else, and knew that I would not. This place had been left to Nature. I stopped the car only because a fallen tree in the road had made the route impassable.

Beyond the driver's side window, half-obscured amongst brambles, stood a broken wooden gate, hinged in studded-iron. The dark grey stone of Alderway was visible from here too and once again I shuddered as an inexplicable coldness crept through me.

I switched off the engine and sat for a moment, listening to the rain ticking against the roof of the car, wondering why I had come here.

I turned to the passenger seat – the seat where you once sat – and fumbled through the rolls of brass-rubbings until I found the family tree that you had created.

The first relatives must have been easy to source:

Simon Tacher (Father)
Geoffrey Tacher (Grandfather)
Edwin Earl Tacher (Great Grandfather)
Henry Jameson Tacher (Great Great Grandfather)

But after that, to unwind history back so far, to the arrival of a French family at Alderway in 1242, must have been painstaking.

The fallow deer came to the lawn again last week; a nervous doe and its slender fawn. They have been away for some days and only stayed a moment before something in the woodland startled them. I thought I saw something in the trees too. As I become weaker, they visit the lawn less and less. In a way, it makes perfect sense. A new pattern.

The cemetery at Alderway is unremarkable if not for the ancient yew-tree that shadows the majority of the graves and keeps the air moist and filled with the scent of damp earth. As I walked beneath its heavy branches and towards the entrance of the church I noticed the grass was not trimmed and that many of the headstones were crumbled and dilapidated. There were no fresh flowers about the graves, nothing to suggest that anyone had been buried here for a long time.

Just before I pulled open the thick mahogany door, I gazed up at the Norman tower of the church. Dark stone against amber-tinted skies.

Then, without reason, I had the strangest feeling that someone was standing directly behind me, on the pathway I had just walked but when I turned to look, there was nothing, only the headstones jutting from the ground like crooked teeth, a crow cawing into the silence and the yew tree, casting dark shadows about the overgrown grass. The sweet scent of jasmine hung in the air.

I wonder now if it was you Caroline, standing there, willing me away from this place one final time.

Inside, the church was musty and cold but a set of strip-lights, hanging far above, cast an orangey glow over the wooden pews and broke the silence with a monotonous hum of electricity.

I strolled down the south transept, towards the altar and the colossal oak cross that hung before the stained windows, conscious of the sound of my step as I went. The flag stones were smooth beneath foot from centuries of wear and, as I reached the altar, I looked down to see the brass image of the knight that you had rubbed onto the tracing paper.

I knelt and gazed into the face peering back at me from behind the shining visor.

Yes, the similarity was too faithful to be anything but an ancestor; the hook of the nose and deep-set eyes; the birth mark about the right eye so keenly etched into the metal. I stood again, this time absorbing the entire image of the knight; sword at centre, clad in well-cut armour. The deep italics engraved above his head looked as though they had been impressed only yesterday:

Here Doth Not Lie
Simone le Tache
1268
The One who made Foole of The Devile

Below these words, and in a separate box that had been carved from the figure's chest, were another group of engravings, perhaps of Arabic or Chinese;

more like symbols than words. I recognised them immediately from your brass rubbings. You had specifically focussed on this section.

I started as a voice sounded behind me.

"Interesting, is it not?"

I turned to see a chaplain dressed in black habit and dog collar smiling on at me with pale blue eyes. I took him to be around sixty and in poor health. He was overweight and his breaths wheezed as he leaned heavily against his wooden stick. When he saw the birthmark to my right eye, something passed over his face that I could not gauge. Something like fear, although it was hard to tell.

"Yes," I agreed, "but it makes no sense. Why should he *not lie* here? I don't get it."

His grip tightened momentarily on his stick as he coughed and wheezed into the silence, but then his smile returned.

"Legend has it", he began, "that Simone le Tache arrived in Alderway in 1252 having travelled from central France. He was not a man of any great wealth and at some point, it is written at least, he sold his soul to the Devil in return for riches. The Devil agreed to secure his wealth but warned him that wherever his body was buried – be it inside or outside the church – that he would take his soul to Hell. Soon afterwards, Le Tache became unexpectedly wealthy but on his death, years later, his family buried him neither inside the church, nor outside."

"They buried him here." He tapped his stick at the stony wall beside him. "Inside the northern wall. So you see, not inside the church, not outside the church.

He cheated the Devil and his soul escaped damnation, hence the writing here on the brass plate."

Silence settled around us, broken only by the buzzing of the strip lights.

"That's a great story," I said, stooping once again to look into the face of Simone le Tache. "Really Great."

"Oh, but that's only the half of it, literally." He prodded his stick towards the ground. "The carpet beside the effigy – pull it up and look underneath. Well, go on."

I knelt down and rolled back the thin red carpet to reveal another brass plate, directly to its right.

"An exact replica," he said. "A perfect mirror image of the original. You see even the words have been mirrored to read backwards."

"That's extraordinary," I said, rubbing my fingers across both smooth surfaces. "But why?"

"Why indeed," he wheezed, hobbling slowly towards the altar. "Why indeed? That is indeed the question."

"There must be a reason," I said, feeling over the cold metal. "The work that has gone into this. The symmetry is perfect."

"Well, the truth is, nobody knows. It is the great mystery of Alderway and in a way it is good. The mystery keeps the place interesting. The congregation has dwindled in recent years and any interest can only be a good thing, I think."

I had stopped listening to him now and was focussed only on the brass images before me, trying to find a fault in the symmetry. The wording: all perfectly reversed. The imprint of Le Tache in his armour, even the intricate flowers on his sword: all flawless in reflection on the corresponding brass plate. Even the Arabic-looking symbols, in the box of their own across the knight's chest: all mirrored exactly.

"I just can't see it," I said. "But there must be a pattern. A reason."

I stood up and gazed down at the images from above, and suddenly there it was.

"The reflection is perfect," I said it aloud. "The symmetry is there. But it's chiral."

"What is chiral?"

"It means the image cannot be perfectly superimposed onto itself. The images look the same, but are different when you put one on top of the other. Wait. I'll be back."

"Slow down, young man. There is all the time," he said, leaning against his stick. "All is well. A mystery can be a mystery. There is no harm to it. Quite the opposite, I think."

But there was no time for dawdling. I knew I was right, as you must have known. I rushed back through the cemetery, beneath the yew, to the car where I found the brass rubbings and your dark-blue wax crayon. I realised then, as I huddled them against my body in the beating rain and made my way back to the church, why you had chosen tracing paper. It was the only way to see, properly.

Once inside, I strode to the brass plates and knelt again.

I unrolled the first brass-rubbing, the one of the knight's face, then pushed it aside. Not that one. Then the next, and the next, until I found the images of the chest portion, where symbols had appeared Arabic or Chinese. There were two rolls of tracing paper, but I chose the one on which you had written, *Mirror Image.*

I laid it on top of the original brass plate and lined up the edges until the square fit perfectly. Then I began to rub across the symbols with the wax crayon, and soon it became clear.

"You see," I said, as I rubbed frantically. "They're not symbols, or letters from another language, but half-letters, English letters. They only become whole when the mirror image is superimposed onto them. It's a mirror image, but you have to put them together to make them whole. Chiral. There, now you see."

I stood back and read the words that now appeared in waxy blue text:

But The Devile will take what is His
and Owne the souls of those who share the Blood
Line of le Tache
And who Step upon this Place.

The atmosphere had changed now and I looked up towards the altar, at the cross. Behind me, the walking stick clicked against stone and a whispery laughter echoed into the silence.

A chill found its way down my neck, tingling to the base of my spine as his voice rasped out.

"I have waited a long time for you. But time is mine. I have all the time. Now who is the fool?"

The deer do not come now. I was right about the pattern. It was inevitable that my deterioration would result in their absence. The roses have died and the shadows in the trees are clearer with each day that passes. The new pattern is easy to understand. My every weakness becomes His every strength. My every loss becomes His gain. He is coming nearer because He knows I am close to the end.

Last night, I had the dream again.

In the dream, I was running from the church, through the beating rain, beneath the yew tree to the car, not looking back. I started the engine and manoeuvred a turn in the road before pulling away. I tried not to look as the old man tapped his cane at my window but something made me look, just as it did that day, and I saw his face again – the face that no one should see.

When I woke, it was to a noise outside on the lawn. I went to the window. The clouds had parted and moonlight cast a silvery light across the grass. Near the rose bed, I could make out the portly figure, resting against His stick, staring back up at me.

No, it is not long now, and He knows.

I will leave this letter by your graveside, Caroline, far from Alderway. I used to believe that, even though you were taken from me, we would meet again some sunny day. But now I know it can never be, because of all that we found at Alderway.

I have one last idea, though it may come to nothing.

Dear Mr Tacher,

Thank you for your letter of 19 September 1985.

May I begin by expressing my regret to hear that you have been ill of health in recent weeks. I wish you a speedy recovery and all the very best for the future.

It is my unfortunate duty to inform you that your request to be buried inside the North Wall of Alderway Church, Berkshire, alongside your ancestor, has been declined by the Council. It is worth mentioning that we receive a number of such letters each year, outlining unusual applications, and that we are not always in a position to provide consent.

You may be aware that Alderway Church has remained vacant of both congregation and minister for some years now, however, it is important to note that the church itself, dating from the early 13th Century, is of Significant Historical Interest and as such is a Listed building. It will not be possible therefore to make any alteration to the building, however small, without an application, and subsequent approval, from the High Court. You may wish to pursue this route, and indeed I enclose papers should you choose to do so, however I would point out that I have never known a request such as this to be authorised by any Court in England.

I am sorry that we have been unable to facilitate your request in this instance.

As I say, I wish you all the best for the future.

Yours faithfully

Brian Jones
Administrative Manager
Berkshire Borough Council

By the Same Author

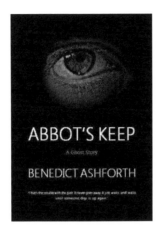

Praise for the ghost novella, Abbot's Keep:

'. . . the horror and suspense starts to be ratcheted up and then gradually builds up speed until the protagonists are overwhelmed in a crescendo of malevolent and inevitable evil. A really entertaining read with a delightful frisson of fear.' *Simon Ball, The Horror HotHouse*

'Ashforth does Edgar Allen Poe and Bram Stoker proud delivering a solid contribution to the literary movement. It is time that the ghost story made a comeback. With writers like Benedict Ashforth writing Abbot's Keep, a revival just might be at hand.' *Matthew J. Barbour of Horror Novel Reviews*

'Reminiscent of Poe, Abbot's Keep by Benedict Ashforth is a haunting novella with unique form and beautiful prose.' *Michael Bailey, HWA Bram Stoker Award Nominee*

'Ashforth builds on the tension and the feeling of unease with each page to revel in a wonderfully tense and unnerving finale.' *Jim Mcleod, Ginger Nuts of Horror*

DARKEST PAST

By the Same Author

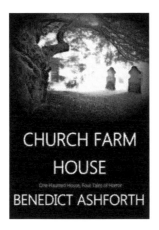

Spanning four decades, the dark history of Church Farm
House is explored within four interlinking horror stories.
Welcome to the nightmare . . .

Coming Soon . . .

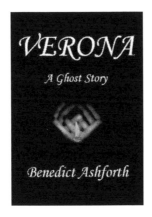

An infertile couple escape to Italy for a short break but soon realise they are not alone, and that a long-forgotten evil has awoken.

DARKEST PAST

About the Author

Benedict Ashforth lives in Dorset, England, with wife, Lynne, and son, Antony.

Benedict was born in Redhill, Surrey, and was schooled at Ampleforth College in North Yorkshire.

benedict2012@hotmail.co.uk

@HorrorFly

Did You Enjoy DARKEST PAST?

Your feedback is immensely important to the author.

For all of your comments – positive or negative – please post your review on www.amazon.com

18747864R00079

Printed in Great Britain
by Amazon